A Family With the Cowboy

A Family With the Cowboy

The Westons of Montana

Elsa Winckler

TULE
PUBLISHING

A Family With the Cowboy
Copyright© 2024 Elsa Winckler
Tule Publishing First Printing February 2025

The Tule Publishing, Inc.

ALL RIGHTS RESERVED

First Publication by Tule Publishing 2024

Cover design by LLewellen Designs

No part of this book may be used or reproduced in any manner whatsoever without written permission except in the case of brief quotations embodied in critical articles and reviews.

This is a work of fiction. Names, characters, places, and incidents are products of the author's imagination or are used fictitiously. Any resemblance to actual events, locales, organizations, or persons, living or dead, is entirely coincidental.

ISBN: 978-1-964703-96-1

Dedication

To Theo, my real-life hero—
thanks for all your support.

Chapter One

SLIGHTLY LIGHTHEADED, LAURA tried to take in everything around her. It was still so surreal, but she was actually here. In Marietta. In Grey's Saloon, to be precise, one of the lovely old buildings on Main Street with a classic Western storefront, like most of the buildings in this part of town.

When she'd entered the bar minutes ago with Maria Baker, her new colleague, who'd met her on her arrival in town today, she had to blink a few times. It was the oldest building in town, Maria had explained. With scarred floorboards, tarnished mirrors, swinging doors, and a balustrade balcony running along the second story, she wouldn't have been surprised if a line of chorus girls had appeared. It was like a scene straight out of a Wild West movie.

She'd read about Marietta's history, of course. Reading had always been her escape, and she'd enjoyed researching everything she could find about the new town she was moving to.

When copper was found in the mountains around Marietta during the late 1800s by mining engineers, the place was flooded by prospectors, miners, and everyone else eager to get rich. Within ten years all mining had stopped, though. Turned out the copper had been more like fool's gold. Many people left, but those who stayed put down roots, raised cattle, and worked the land. Today Marietta was a thriving community of ranchers with many shops and other commercial enterprises.

Smiling, Maria lifted her beer. "Welcome to Marietta. So, tell me, what made you decide to move here from Missoula? Don't get me wrong, I love our small town, but it's much smaller than what you're used to."

"Last October, my friend Maisy and I stopped here when we were on our way to Yellowstone National Park during school break and before she got married. For me, it was love at first sight. We stayed at Annie's, the B&B, and I just immediately fell in love with Copper Mountain and the town. Annie and her husband were so enthusiastic about everything, we ended up staying two more days to soak up all Marietta has to offer—from walking down Main Street, admiring all the beautiful storefronts, to eating too many chocolates from the chocolate shop, to skating on Miracle Lake."

"It's charming, I agree, but still a huge change, isn't it? What about your family?" Maria immediately held up a hand and grinned apologetically. "Sorry, small-town inquisitiveness. You don't have to answer me."

A strange tingle ran down Laura's back. Was someone

looking at her? Trying to ignore it, she focused on Maria. She was probably just tired, and that's why she was imagining things.

"I lost my mom when I was eight and Dad passed away at the beginning of last year. So when Maisy got married in November and moved away to Los Angeles and I saw the ad about the post at Marietta Elementary School, it was like a sign telling me it was time for a change."

Maria lifted her beer. "And then you got the job. You were by far the best candidate."

Shaking her head, Laura laughed. "I still find it difficult to believe I got the job and that I'm here. There was nothing to keep me in Missoula. Dad's house was sold and his estate finally wrapped up. I quickly found someone to take over the lease of my apartment. Another colleague who was helping out temporarily at school was looking for a permanent post and the rest just fell into place. And here I am. I have to admit, while driving here, I've been questioning my sanity! I like my comfort zones and this move"—she gestured with her hands—"kinda plucked me right out of it!"

"And what about a significant other? You're so beautiful. Don't tell me you don't have a someone special?" Maria laughed. "Again, sorry. But everyone, and I mean everyone, is going to ask you that question."

Laura grinned. She liked her new colleague. "No one special, I'm happy to say. I'm not really relationship material, my last boyfriend told me. Men are so needy—at least the ones I've been dating. And oh, my word, do they carry baggage around. They either have mommy issues or daddy issues or issues with exes. The last guy I dated for a few weeks still had hang-ups about his previous girlfriend. Don't get me wrong. I know we all have things we have to deal with, but you don't have to talk about it all the time."

Maria laughed. "I think you've been dating the wrong men."

"Maybe, but right now my goal is to enjoy life as a happily single gal and not get entangled in any man's drama. I like my freedom and independence."

Maria's eyes twinkled. "In that case, you should steer clear of Janice O'Sullivan."

"Who is Janice?"

"The self-appointed matchmaker of Marietta. You've met Annie and Craig. She's Craig's godmother and according to the gossip mill, it's all Janice's doing that they're together. The fact that Craig's cousin, Riley, married Mitch, Annie's brother, and that Vivian, Annie's sister, married Aiden O'Sullivan, also a cousin of Craig's, are, according to rumors, also because of our Janice's matchmaking skills."

Alarmed, Laura shook her head. "I'll make sure to stay far away from her. I have absolutely no plans to marry anyone."

"You don't have a thing for cowboys?" Maria grinned. "That's usually the reason single women move to Marietta nowadays. Especially after the latest hit television show about

Montana."

Laura shuddered. "No cowboy for me, thank you. I prefer the men I date to drive a car, not a truck, and I like men clean, not all sweaty and reeking of animals."

Maria leaned back in her chair, her eyes twinkling. "Well, then, this is going to be interesting. There is a cowboy sitting behind you who hasn't taken his eyes off of you ever since we sat down. Really interesting. You see, he's one of . . ."

"Maria!" someone called out and a man hurried closer.

Maria's face lit up and she jumped to her feet. "It's my husband. He's been away…" That was as far as she got. Then the newcomer grabbed her and kissed her soundly.

Laughing, Maria finally pushed him away and introduced Laura. "My husband, Luis. Luis, a new colleague, Laura Anderson. She's taking over from Mrs. Denton, who just retired."

Luis smiled and greeted her. "You're starting mid-term?"

Laura nodded. "Yes, I am. Maria has been so helpful today."

He put an arm around his wife. "She is a wonderful teacher. Have you eaten yet?"

"We've just arrived," said Maria. "I'm treating Laura to dinner, but you're welcome to join us."

Just then a harried-looking waitress arrived. "What can I get you?"

They ordered and Laura excused herself. She needed

time to take a breath and give Maria and Luis a few minutes alone.

As she walked away, she turned her head ever so slightly to look at the table next to theirs. A pair of amber eyes, the color of the triple-distilled whiskey her dad had always preferred, met hers. Her heart kicked against her ribs. Wow, a real-life cowboy, if the hat resting on his knee was anything to go by.

Quickly she moved toward the bathroom, the tingle down her spine telling her he was still looking her way.

In the small room, she quickly washed her hands. Inhaling shakily, she stared at herself before combing her fingers through her longish bob. It was Friday, and Monday would be her first working day as a teacher at Marietta Elementary School. She'd left Missoula early this morning and had arrived just before lunch. It was only about a four-hour drive. Along the way she'd stopped a few times, so she wasn't really tired, but she was going to excuse herself after dinner.

She was staying at Annie's for a few days before moving into the rental house she'd been fortunate to find on Collier Street. Her furniture and books would arrive sometime next week, she'd been told. At some point she'd probably look into buying a house, but she wanted to take her time doing that.

Getting tingles down her back because a cowboy was looking at her was so not something she had time for right now. Squaring her shoulders, she opened the bathroom door.

As she stepped out, she bumped into a solid body. Earthy tones of man and musk swirled around her. Immediately, all her senses jumped to attention.

"Sorry," she muttered, and tried to escape, but the person in front of her wasn't moving.

"Excuse me," she tried again and, irritated, she pushed against him. Big mistake. Her hands landed on a warm, muscled torso. They both froze. She looked up. It was the same cowboy she'd caught staring at her minutes earlier.

Those whiskey-colored eyes didn't blink. "You passing through town?" a deep voice rumbled.

She shook her head.

One side of his mouth lifted ever so slightly. "Pity." His head dropped. "Something tells me you may not be so averse to sweaty cowboys as you think."

Before she could catch her breath, he'd turned away and was walking through the swinging doors into the night.

Blinking, she steadied herself against the wall. Oh, my. If the first cowboy she met in town had this effect on her, it was a good thing she was living and working in town and would hopefully not run into any on a daily basis.

She quickly made her way back to the table. Her whole body was still tingling.

HAYDEN GOT OFF his horse. He'd been out with his two

brothers since early morning, looking for stragglers. They'd probably join him soon. As he tied the reins to the gate at the small family graveyard at the foot of the hill, he inhaled the cold air and looked around him.

He would forever be grateful for a great-grandfather who had picked this piece of land and settled here. To the southeast lay Yellowstone National Park, and from here, you could feast your eyes on the snowcapped peaks of the Absaroka Range of the Rockies. To the northeast lay the Gallatin River. His family's blood and tears had been spilled to work this land full of wildlife, hot springs, and roaming cattle.

Since the previous Friday night, he'd been out of sorts. It was Monday, ten days later, but he was still restless. Since he'd seen the blonde. Since she'd touched him. Since he'd inhaled her flowery scent. Since something had stirred inside of him, for the first time in a long time. What the hell had gotten into him, he didn't know, but for one moment he'd thought if she was passing through town, he could take her to the Graff Hotel and have sex with her.

Muttering and cussing, he opened the gate and entered. Sex wasn't something he'd thought about for two long years. Damn it, he didn't have time for this. He had a ranch to run.

There was something in the way she'd held her head, the way her hair swung over her shoulders when she moved, that had caught his eye, and once he'd noticed her he couldn't seem to look away. She was gorgeous. Honey-blonde hair fell to her shoulders in a straight bob. His fingers had itched. Literally. All he could think about was running his fingers through her tresses. And when she stood up and he saw those long, well-formed, jeans-clad legs, there was a moment he was worried he'd slobber all over the table.

The last time he'd felt such an immediate attraction had been when he'd met his late wife, Madeline.

With his eyes on the last two tombstones, he walked past the graves of his great-grandfather and great-grandmother, his grandpa and his nana, and past his dad's until he reached the spot between his wife's and his brother's grave.

As always when he came here, the permanent band that had been around his chest for the past five years tightened. There was no getting over grief, he'd learned over time. You simply had to learn to live with the pain that would forever be a part of you.

Cancer had taken Madeline, his beautiful, loving wife, two years ago. He'd thought nothing could ever be worse than losing his brother, but then Madeline fell ill. Luke, their son, had only been six at the time. Hayden had no idea how he would cope, how to be a dad and a mom to their energetic and strong-willed little boy. He still didn't.

And looking at his son, it was clear he wasn't doing a great job. Since his mom had passed away, Luke had changed from a laughing, happy child to a silent one. His smile was gone. He rarely spoke. He'd started school just after Madeline passed and was now in second grade. Hayden tried talking to him about his day during dinner, but all he usually got was a shrug, so he had no idea how Luke was coping.

His siblings had their meals at the big homestead where he and Luke—and until two years ago, Madeline—lived. Isabella, the wife of one of the oldest cowboys on the ranch, Ricardo, had been cooking for them ever since he could remember. They all enjoyed each other's company; it was also one of the few times he got to see his son. He would have to get creative and find another time to talk to Luke.

He should probably also go and see the teacher, but on a busy ranch there never seemed to be time.

Sighing, his eyes moved to the other grave and lingered over the words engraved on the cold marble. *Walker Weston—you were loved*, followed by the date of his brother's birth and the date of the accident in which they'd lost him—February 11th, exactly five years ago.

And as always happened when he came here, the events of that fateful night flashed before his eyes. He'd been driving. Both of his other brothers, Becket and Cooper, as well as their sister, Willow, were in the car. Although they seldom talked about the accident, he knew his siblings were all blaming themselves for what happened too. The bottom line was, though, he was the one behind the wheel. He was responsible.

If only... Looking up toward the mountains, he swallowed against the lump in his throat. Of course, none of the if-onlys would bring back their brother, with his big laugh and kind eyes. Not one.

A soft footfall behind him had him turning his head. Willow was approaching and behind her, their faces grave, were Becket and Cooper. They'd also arrived on horseback; he'd been too preoccupied to hear them.

Wordlessly, they joined him and, for long minutes, the four of them stood quietly next to the grave, remembering their brother.

It was bitterly cold, the world around them robed in white, but none of them seemed to be aware of it.

Hayden finally cleared his throat. "From weather reports, the cold weather isn't changing anytime soon. We still have enough surplus hay for the winter feeding?" It was easier to talk about things that needed to be done.

Becket nodded. "There should be more than enough. I'm on my way to check." With a wave, he turned away.

"Have you seen Luke?" Hayden asked his sister and Cooper.

He caught the look between them. "No, I haven't," Willow said. She put a hand on Hayden's arm. "Try talking to him instead of shouting, will you?" She cocked her head. "You okay? You seemed to be even grumpier than usual this week. Anything happened?"

"I'm fine," he just about snarled.

Shrugging, she moved away to follow Becket. "See you later." She stopped and turned. "By the way, Mom phoned.

She said she's texted everyone, but you haven't responded. We're all invited to dinner tomorrow evening. Or rather, late afternoon. Mom wants us there at six."

Hayden frowned. "Whatever for? And what about Sunday?" Since their mom moved to the family house in town a year ago, Sunday lunch at her place was a standing, nonnegotiable date.

Willow smiled. "Sunday lunch is still on, sorry. Apparently, she's getting a new neighbor and wants us to help welcome the person to Marietta."

Hayden cussed and rubbed his face. He didn't have time for a damn dinner in the middle of the week.

"I also haven't seen Luke," Cooper muttered as he waved and left.

Hayden grimaced. If his siblings' reactions were anything to go by, Luke had again forgotten to do his chores. Something had obviously changed or happened in his son's life over the past few days. The question was, what? And how did he persuade Luke to talk to him?

Damn it, on days like this, he wished he could ask Madeline how to handle the situation. Whatever he tried to do, he seemed to make matters worse.

It wasn't as if Luke had many chores, but helping out, doing your bit on a big ranch, had been instilled in all of them since they could walk. And Luke had been helpful, even doing more than what he should until recently.

And okay, Willow was right. He had been shouting at his

A FAMILY WITH THE COWBOY

son. He didn't mean to raise his voice, but he was at his wits' end and didn't know how to get through to Luke.

By the time he reached the homestead, it was nearly dark. Still muttering, he got off his horse. "Luke!" he called out. Their cook Isabella also looked after Luke, but his son was seldom in the house.

Silence.

"Jessie!" he tried. Usually, the border collie responded.

A bark from inside the barn confirmed where Jessie was. And, hopefully, Luke would be close by. Jessie's water bowl was almost empty, he noticed, as he entered the barn.

Jessie saw Hayden and, barking joyously, she ran toward him. Luke was lying on hay in the loft, apparently still unaware of what was going on around him.

Hayden walked closer. "What are you doing?"

Luke quickly looked up, but it was clear he was still somewhere inside the pages of the book he'd been reading. Only after blinking a few times did he seem to realize where he was. Jumping up, he stashed the book in the front of his jacket. "Sorry, Dad. On my way."

"Wait," Hayden stopped him. "What the hell's going on, Luke? Over the last week you haven't been doing your chores."

"'Cause I was reading," Luke said.

"Reading?" Sighing, Hayden rubbed his face. "This is a ranch. Everyone has a job to do. Do you understand that?"

"Yes, but I . . ."

"No buts, Luke. I don't want to talk about this again."

With that stubborn pure Weston look, Luke glared at him. "My teacher says books are the most important thing in the world. They take you to places you can never otherwise go and I—"

"Your teacher?" Remembering Mrs. Denton, Hayden frowned. She was married to a rancher, so she should know how important ranch work was.

"Yes, she reads to us every day. It's my favorite thing." Just for a moment, something of the joy that had always been in his son's eyes shone through, but then his shoulders dropped and he looked miserable again.

Hayden sighed. There was no getting through to the boy. "You remember what I always tell you about ranching?"

Luke nodded. "We are stewards of the land. It's our 'sponsibility."

"Exactly. And everyone must do their bit."

"Yes, Dad," he muttered, as he climbed down the stairs.

Hayden rubbed his face. Well, tomorrow first thing, he was going to see Mrs. Denton. He couldn't remember her ever reading to them all those years ago, but maybe things had changed.

Muttering, he walked toward the homestead. He didn't have time to go into town once, let alone twice in one day. Yes, it was winter and things were slower, but there was still a lot of work. With temperatures dropping, the cattle needed more feed to maintain their body heat. Then there was the problem they were having with elks, one that nobody seemed to be able to find a solution to. On top of that, they had to deal with the influx of people wanting to buy previously family-owned ranches because they'd watched a damn television show. They had money, but no idea what ranching meant. His blood started boiling at the mere thought.

But before he could solve other problems, he had to talk to Mrs. Denton.

Chapter Two

LAURA INHALED THE crisp, cold air as she got out of her car. It was already Tuesday, her second week in Marietta, and she was excited to start the new day.

After only a week in town she'd met Carol Bingley, the town gossip, at the pharmacy and she'd heard about Carol's friend, Betty, who was the police dispatcher. Even though she'd been warned, she had been quite taken aback by the way Carol questioned her about every single aspect of her life. Fortunately, the pharmacy had been busy and she'd managed to escape without answering the nosy woman.

She'd also met Janice O'Sullivan last week at Annie's when Annie and Craig had invited their whole family so that she could meet them.

As Maria had predicted, Janice immediately wanted to know whether she had a boyfriend. Shaking her head, Laura grabbed her bag and the basket full of books from her car. It had been lovely to meet Vivian, Annie's sister, her husband, Aiden, and also Riley, who was married to Mitch, Annie's brother. She was, though, steering clear of Janice, however charming the older woman looked.

She liked men, yes, but the few relationships she'd tried had left her wary and weary. Men were either overbearing or clingy, neither of which she found particularly endearing or sexy. Dating would be okay, but getting involved with a man? Not so much.

And at least she now knew a few more people in Marietta.

The moving van with her furniture would be arriving tonight, she'd been told. Although she'd enjoyed her stay with Annie, she couldn't wait to be in her own place. She'd only seen a picture of the house she would be renting before she'd arrived in Marietta, but when she saw the beautiful house, a traditional rustic style in stone and reclaimed wood, it was love at first sight.

According to the realtor, the owners were looking to sell, so one of the first things she wanted to do when she had time was to go to the bank.

She wouldn't be able to do much unpacking before the weekend, but hopefully she'd be able to get at least one bedroom ready during the coming week.

Over the past weekend she'd picked up the key to the house the real estate agent had left with one of the neighbors…Arlene, if she remembered correctly. The older woman was very nice and friendly and had invited her to contact her at any time if she needed any help. If she couldn't help, Arlene said, one of her four children should be able to. She'd probably meet the rest of the family in time.

The key had made it possible to move most of the things she had with her to the house the previous evening. The electricity and water had also been turned on and the house was ready for her.

This morning she'd had her last fabulous breakfast with Annie. Being served a hot breakfast before she had to go to work was definitely something she was going to miss dearly.

Hitching her bag over her shoulder, Laura walked toward her classroom. It was still early. She had about an hour before her second graders arrived, but she loved to get everything ready before they turned up. They were discussing multiple-meaning words this week and she had made several posters she wanted to put up.

After taking off her coat, she took *The Lorax*, one of Dr. Seuss's books, from the pile in her tote bag and left it on her desk. She'd just finished reading it to the kids. They'd enjoyed the story, and she hoped some of them would realize how important it was to protect their beautiful environment. And maybe a few would also understand something about the consequences of mass production from the story.

Luke Weston, one of the kids in her class, especially seemed to love the stories she'd been reading to them at the end of each day. He always listened so intently, she'd asked if he would like to borrow the books. It was the first time she'd seen him smile. She'd told him he could have this one, too, when she'd finished reading it to the class.

Meeting the kids' parents was important to her and she'd

sent out letters last week, inviting them to come and see her after school. Most parents had responded, but she hadn't heard anything from Luke's mom or dad.

There hadn't yet been time to sit down and read everything about the kids in her class. She'd been frantically trying to catch up on the work that still had to be done. As she'd discovered since her arrival, Mrs. Denton hadn't been feeling well since before Christmas and it was clear the poor woman hadn't been able to do much with the kids.

Hopefully, she'd soon know everything there was to know about all the children. Maybe then she'd be able to figure out why Luke Weston looked so unhappy.

Humming, she rummaged through her basket, looking for the book she wanted to read to the class this week. Frowning, she emptied the basket, but the book wasn't there. It had probably fallen out on her way to school.

Grabbing her coat again, she rushed to the door, and while looking down at the buttons of her coat, she flung it open, already moving toward her car. But instead of moving forward, she was abruptly stopped by an unmoving object. She reached out to steady herself and her hands landed on a warm body. Familiar earthy tones of man and musk penetrated her befuddled brain.

Before she could figure out what had happened, big hands closed around her upper arms.

"What the hell?" the same voice rumbled.

Still stunned, she looked up, and up, not wanting to see

what she already knew she would see. It was the cowboy from the previous Friday night. A frown appeared between his eyes as recognition slowly dawned on him.

Eventually, she registered her hands were still spread out over his muscled upper body. Quickly dropping them, she stepped back. "May I help you?" she asked, trying not to look as flustered as she was feeling.

Still frowning, he looked up at the number above the door. "You…you were in Grey's Saloon last Friday night?"

Nodding briefly, she lifted her chin. "May I help you?" she asked again.

"Isn't this Mrs. Denton's classroom?"

"Mrs. Denton retired at the end of January. I'm the new second-grade teacher."

His mouth opened and closed a few times. "Why the hell didn't I know that?"

"Is there a reason you should know?"

"Hell, yes!" he said through clenched teeth. "My son is in this class."

"Your son?"

"Luke. Luke Weston."

Ah. Finally, many things made sense. "Well, Mr. Weston, if you or your wife had taken the time to read the letters I sent you last week, you would know that, one"—she ticked on her fingers—"your son has a new teacher, and, two, I would like to make an appointment to see both of you to talk about Luke."

He frowned. "Why?"

"I would prefer it if your wife…"

"My wife, Miss Whoever-you-are, is dead. If you want to talk about Luke, you talk to me."

It was her turn to open and close her mouth a few times. Inhaling deeply, she put out a hand. "I'm sorry, Mr. Weston. I'm Laura Anderson and I'm your son's new teacher. Do you have a few minutes?"

He ignored her hand. "No, I don't have a few minutes. I have a ranch to run. I'm here to tell you not to give Luke more books to read. He's neglected his chores, something he's never done before. I caught him in the barn yesterday afternoon, reading a damn book!"

The way the big man was carrying on, you'd think his son was committing a federal crime. No wonder poor Luke looked so unhappy.

"You should be pleased about that, not mad."

"I'm not…" he bellowed before he caught himself. Rubbing his face, he turned on his heel. "I don't have time for this."

"Mr. Weston," she called out. "We really should talk."

He stopped and glared at her over his shoulder. "You wanna talk to me? You come and see me." And off he stomped.

Completely stunned, she stared after him.

"What on earth have you done to Hayden Weston?" Maria asked from behind Laura.

Laura threw up her hands. "I have no idea. He stormed in here this morning, looking for Mrs. Denton. He didn't even know his son had a different teacher. And I've been sending letters to them, trying to see him or his wife…"

Mariah inhaled sharply.

Laura grimaced. "I've just heard his wife died. I didn't know…"

Mariah patted her shoulder. "So, you haven't gotten to the kids' reports yet?"

Laura shook her head. "There hasn't been time. It's no excuse, I know. I'll make time tonight."

Maria grinned. "Don't beat yourself up. Moving to another town, taking over a class mid-term—none of it is easy. Well, you've been invited to his ranch. You should go and see him. It's a beautiful place."

"At least I now know why poor Luke looks so unhappy. With a grumpy father like that, anyone would be."

Maria chuckled. "By the way, he's the one who was checking you out in Grey's Saloon the other night."

Turning away before the heat creeping up her neck gave her away, Laura huffed. "So not interested, thank you very much. I've left something in my car. Excuse me."

Maria's laugh followed her all the way down the hall.

HAYDEN STOPPED IN front of his mother's place with

screeching tires. He and Luke were late for dinner. Luke hadn't done his chores. Again. Tired, irritated, and worried about his son, Hayden got out of his truck. He had to shout at his son. Again. The last thing he wanted to do was have dinner with his mother. She didn't miss a thing, so she'd know right away something was wrong. It wasn't as if she'd pester him. Oh, no, his mother was way too subtle and devious to do that. She'd smile and prod and ask questions ever so gently until she'd get everything out of him and/or Luke before the end of the evening.

As they walked toward his mom's house, he noticed a moving truck and a car parked in front of the house next door. The house had been standing empty since before Christmas, so he was glad to see someone would be moving in next door to his mom again.

At seventy, she was still a force to be reckoned with, but she was getting older, whether they wanted to acknowledge it or not.

Before they'd reached the porch, the front door opened and the rest of his family filed out.

"I was wondering where you two were," his mom said as she reached them. She held out her arms and hugged Luke. Hayden got a kiss on the cheek. "We are on our way to welcome my new neighbor and see where we can help before we have dinner. Hopefully, she'll be able to join us. Such a lovely woman, I really hope . . ." She stopped speaking and gave Hayden "The Look," as he and his siblings referred to this particular stare of their mom's. "Something is wrong…"

"We're fine, Mom," he interrupted. "I saw the moving truck next door. I assume that's the new neighbor you want us to welcome?"

His mother's gaze roamed another second over his face before she turned to walk toward the neighbor's house. "Yes, the Gearings' house. Lydia moved to the senior citizen facilities before Christmas and the house has been empty since then."

"So you've met the neighbor?" Willow asked as they all followed their mother.

"Yes, the real estate agent left the key with me over the weekend, and she picked it up. A stunning girl. Becket, maybe she's the one to stop you from breaking any more hearts around town. Carol Bingley went on and on about poor Susanne this morning. Apparently, she's walking around town, crying, because you've dumped her."

"She wanted to look at rings," Becket muttered. "You know how I feel about that."

"That's what happens when you take out a woman and wine and dine her for a few weeks." Willow chuckled. "I don't know why you're so surprised every time."

"If that's how it works, how come you're not getting married?" Becket asked Willow.

Willow glared at him. "You know why. It's bad enough worrying about you lot. I can't handle anyone else's drama."

Their mother smiled and patted Willow's shoulder.

"You've inherited your Irish grandma's sense of knowing what's going on in other people's minds. It's a blessing, not a curse."

Willow pursed her lips. "It's a curse, Mom, believe me."

At that moment the front door opened, and two men stepped out.

"Thank you so much for all your help," a woman from somewhere inside the house said.

The men greeted them as they left, but Hayden had frozen. He'd heard that voice before.

Luke inhaled deeply before he rushed forward. "Miss Anderson!" he called out, and the next moment, she appeared in the doorway.

She was wearing jeans and a snug T-shirt that lovingly hugged beautiful breasts. Her hair had been taken up in a bun, but most of it had escaped already. She was barefoot, with her toenails painted pink. A fist of desire so intense that Hayden lost his breath in one swoosh caught him in the solar plexus.

Luke grabbed her hand. "Grandma, this is my new teacher," he said, and, beaming, he turned around to look at all of them.

Chapter Three

LAURA WAS SO stunned, she just stared at the faces in front of her. She hadn't been expecting anyone, and she probably looked awful. Arlene was her neighbor, that she knew, but who were these other people and why were Hayden Weston and his son also on her porch? Grandma, Luke had said. So this…?

Arlene smiled. "Ah, so you're the new teacher Luke can't stop talking about? I should've made the connection." She motioned to the other people. "My children, Laura. That's Willow—she makes beautiful art, if I have to say so myself. And that one is Becket, a notorious womanizer. I'm sure you've already heard that, but he actually has a heart of gold, as you will see when he's with his dogs, Harper, Jack, and Sadie. This is Connor, happier talking to animals than people. He has so many dogs, I can't remember all the names. And the grumpy one here is Hayden, my oldest. His dear Madeline passed away two years ago. And you know Luke. We're here to help and to hopefully persuade you to have dinner with us afterwards?"

Laura was deeply grateful that the older woman was talking, because, for a few moments, she couldn't even think, let alone string logical words together. Every single brain cell she had had ceased to function.

Hayden Weston was here. On her porch. And within minutes, he'd be inside her house. She'd thought she had time before seeing him again. To prepare herself for those amber eyes, that penetrating look, the strange currents in the air when he was near. Here he was, though, whether she was ready or not.

By the time Arlene stopped talking, a few of her brain cells seemed to have recovered. Quickly pushing her feet into her shoes she'd left next to the door, she smiled and walked out on to the porch. "Thank you so much, but it's not necessary. Except for the bed, most of the furniture has been placed where I want it. Thanks, really, but I—"

But that was as far as she got. In the nicest possible way, Arlene moved her to the side and motioned to her children to follow her. "Nonsense, dear. You work during the day. Besides, you're such a slip of a thing, you'll need a hand moving the bed. And here are three muscled boys who are willing to help. Let them help you with that, and Willow and I will unpack things in the kitchen."

Boys. The three Weston brothers were tall, muscled, ridiculously attractive men. "Boys" was so not the word to describe them.

Luke tugged at her hand. Dazed, she looked down. She hadn't realized Luke was still holding on to her.

"Grandma always gets her way," he said, clearly mimicking one of the grown-ups. "So you may as well do as she says."

Everyone chuckled.

"Um…I…you…" Laura stuttered, but by this time everyone had already moved inside her house.

Willow grinned. "Luke is so right. Let's do this. What do you want where?"

Acutely conscious of Hayden's gaze still on her, she tried to think. She'd thought she'd have to plan what she wanted to go where and then she'd figure out who she could ask to help her move the furniture.

"If I could make a suggestion?" Arlene smiled. "Which room are you going to make your bedroom? Let's start with moving the bed to that room so that you can make it. I'm a firm believer if your bed is made, the rest will be easy. And if you can show Willow and me where the boxes are you want in the kitchen, we can start unpacking for you?"

Groaning out loud, Laura laughed. "Okay, thank you, but on one condition. I'll use an hour of your time and not a minute more, okay? There really is no rush to unpack everything tonight."

"You heard her, boys." Arlene grinned. "Come on, Willow. Let's see what you and I can accomplish in an hour."

Luke tugged at her hand again and she crouched down. His eyes were shining, and he was smiling. "What can I do?" he asked shyly.

"Tell you what," she smiled back. "Would you like to unpack some books for me?"

His grin widened. "Yes! Where?"

Jumping up, she steered him toward a bookcase and a box. "I can sort them out later, but if you can put them in here, it will be easier for me later. Think you can do that?"

"Yes, I'm eight," he said proudly, and kneeled next to the box. His eyes widened when he saw the book lying at the top. "This is also one by Dr. Seuss?" he asked in awe and picked up the book.

"Yes, he wrote a number of books…"

"Where do you want the bed?" Hayden asked behind her, his voice anything but friendly.

Luke's smile slipped and, ignoring the gruff voice behind her, she leaned closer to the boy. "If you want to, you can also just sit and read. I can put the books away later," she said softly. A ghost of a smile returned.

Fed up with the big cowboy, she turned around and glared at him before she walked past him to the furniture in the middle of the room. Smiling at Cooper and Becket, she pointed toward the big double bed she'd bought just before she'd moved. "If we can move this to the last room down the hall? It has an en suite bathroom and doors leading to the back garden. I think that's where I'll make my bedroom."

Hayden moved past her to help his brothers, leaving the whiff of musk she'd picked up on before in his wake. Oh, my goodness. What was up with her and the big cowboy?

Tonight, he was without a hat and wore black jeans and a T-shirt under a leather jacket. The jacket he'd removed as they'd entered the house. Tall, dark, sinfully handsome…Flustered, she turned away to find Arlene's amused gaze on her.

She hastily picked up a box. A very heavy one, she discovered seconds later as she staggered forward.

A big hand cut in front of her and took the box from her as if it weighed next to nothing. "We're here to help. Ask, damn it," Hayden bit out.

"I had it," she snapped.

Amber eyes rested on her for a mere second, but she could feel it down to her very soles. This was going to be the longest hour of her life.

IT WAS NEARLY two hours later before they all finally sat down around his mother's kitchen table. Everyone had a plate of food in front of them and the adults, a glass of wine. Luke had milk.

Hayden watched his mom as she lifted her glass. "To Laura. May your stay in Marietta be everything that you've hoped for."

Laura smiled as she also lifted her glass. "Thanks to all you Westons, I'll probably be able to finish unpacking by tomorrow. Thank you, thank you." She smiled at everyone around the table, except at him.

Luke had made sure he sat right next to Laura. His eyes were drooping, and he'd probably fall asleep soon.

"Luke and I are just going to eat and leave, Mom," Hayden said.

"Can't I stay with Grandma?" Luke asked sulkily.

"You have school tomorrow, big guy," his grandma said. "But we'll arrange a visit soon."

"'Kay," Luke muttered. "Can I read when I visit, Grandma?"

His mother frowned. "Of course, you can read when you visit. And I sincerely hope you're able to read anytime you want to."

"Dad yells when I read."

Laura glared at him and everyone else looked stunned.

Hayden swore under his breath. "That's not what—" he tried.

"Hayden, please tell me you don't do that?" his mom interrupted him, her eyebrows raised.

"He's neglecting his chores," Hayden said.

His mother smiled slowly. "I see. So, he's reading instead of doing his chores?"

"That is not something to smile about," Hayden snapped, ignoring the snickering coming from the direction of his brothers.

"Indeed," said his mother, her eyes full of mirth. "I do recall, though, another time when another little boy was caught reading behind the barn instead of doing his chores."

Luke's eyes widened. "Who, Grandma?"

His mom patted Hayden's shoulder. "This guy, Luke. Your dad. He loved reading—"

"That was a long time ago," Hayden interrupted his mother. "Eat up, Luke. We have to leave soon."

"Yes, Dad," Luke muttered, casting his eyes down.

Laura leaned and murmured something to him. Luke flashed her a smile before he began to eat his food.

Ignoring him, Laura smiled in the direction of his brothers. "So, tell me about your ranch. As I drove here, I saw wide-open spaces on either side of the road. I assume the land belongs to ranchers?"

Becket grinned. "Yes, you'd be right. We're, for instance, the fifth-generation Westons on this ranch. Hayden took over when Dad died and when Walker, Coop, and I finished our studies, we joined the family business."

Hayden glared at Becket. Why the hell did Becket have to mention Walker?

Laura frowned. "Who is Walker?"

Becket's smile slipped.

"He was my second oldest," their mother said softly. "We lost him five years ago in an accident."

"I'm so sorry," Laura said, her eyes bright. "That must have been hard for all of you."

For a few minutes it was silent around the table.

Laura cleared her throat, trying to think of something to

say to change the atmosphere. "Five generations of Westons. How extraordinary. I've read quite a bit about Marietta's earlier years, but would love to know more about the history of the surrounding ranches as well."

"If you let me take you to dinner, we can talk history." Becket's grin was back.

Laura chuckled. "What did your mom call you? A notorious womanizer? I can see why. But seeing that I'm forewarned, I should be safe. Dinner sounds nice, thanks."

Before Hayden's stunned eyes, his brother exchanged telephone numbers with his son's gorgeous teacher.

Laura leaned forward. "Cooper, what is your role on the ranch?"

Becket smiled and slapped Cooper on the back. "Coop is our horse whisperer. As if he doesn't have enough to do, he also works with abused horses on the ranch, and all stray animals seem to find their way to him."

"Sounds wonderful." Laura sighed. "I had a dog as a little girl and would love to get one again. We should talk. So, what else do you do?"

"Hayden here is actually the mastermind behind the way we do things on the ranch. You should talk to him," Willow said.

Blue eyes turned in his direction.

Hayden was happy to see Luke had finished his dinner, but he wasn't sure how to feel about the fact that his son was comfortable enough to lean against Laura, his eyes drooping.

She had an arm around him. It was all too much. He had to get out of here.

He put down his knife and fork. His mom was an amazing cook, but he had no idea what he'd eaten tonight or what it tasted like. He was furious. About what exactly, he wasn't sure, but he needed to get away before he said or did something he'd regret.

Wiping his mouth with his napkin, he got up. "Thanks, Mom. I think Luke and I will be going. Laura..." He nodded in her direction. "Luke..." But Luke was now fast asleep, leaning against Laura.

"Luke, buddy," he called out.

"He's sleeping." Laura glared at him. "I'll carry him to the car." Before Hayden could move, she was up and had Luke in her arms.

"He's too big for you to carry. I'll take him." He stepped forward, but Laura was already walking toward the front door.

Muttering softly, he grabbed his car keys, his coat, and her coat before following her outside. It didn't help his mood that his family burst out laughing the minute he'd left the kitchen.

Laura was waiting next to his truck. He put her coat around her shoulders before he bent to take Luke from her.

"I've got him," she murmured, pulling Luke closer.

He opened the door of his truck so that she could set Luke into his booster seat. She stroked her fingers lightly down his son's cheek once before she stepped back so that he could strap the boy safely in for the drive home.

The top of her T-shirt had been pushed down while she'd carried Luke and he caught a glimpse of a milky-white curve of a breast before she straightened her clothes.

"Thank you." His throat was strangely tight.

She slipped her arms into her coat. "He's only eight. If he falls asleep, you should carry him, not wake him up to walk on his own," she scolded.

"Is it part of your job as a teacher to tell parents how to raise their children?" he snapped as he closed the door.

She sighed as she stepped back. "I'm not…" Her foot caught on something, and the next moment, she was falling forward.

He grabbed her and her soft, curvy body ended up plastered against him.

"I'm sorry," she said, sounding out of breath. "I tripped." She pushed against his chest as she steadied herself. They both froze again like they had the previous two times they'd touched.

"This is the third time you've put your hands on me," he said, combing her hair out of her face. "You think you can keep doing that and I won't respond?"

Gasping indignantly, she pulled away quickly. "Don't be ridiculous. The previous two times, you walked into me, and just now, I stumbled—"

"Really? You keep telling yourself that." Without looking

in her direction again, he got into his truck. What the hell had gotten into him? Muttering, he stepped on the pedal, forcing himself not to look in the rearview mirror.

He should stay the hell away from Luke's teacher.

Chapter Four

BY FRIDAY AFTERNOON, as Laura was driving down Main Street, she was still ticked off. She hadn't "put her hands" on Hayden-freaking-Weston, as he'd described it. All three times were accidents. There was no way she'd willingly touch such a cranky, difficult guy. Granted, like his two brothers, he was drop-dead gorgeous—a woman would have to be dead not to notice—but the man managed to push all her wrong buttons.

He was making his poor son's life miserable. Yes, he'd lost his wife, but that didn't give him the right to make everyone else around him unhappy.

She parked her car in front of the bank, close to all the stops she had to make. Her cupboards and fridge were bare, so she needed food. And if she wasn't mistaken, she'd caught a glimpse of what looked like a yarn shop between the pharmacy and Marietta Western Wear when she drove down Main Street the previous week. At the time, it hadn't been opened yet. But hopefully, the owner had settled in by now.

Knitting and crocheting were both crafts she loved doing, but since the decision to move to Marietta, Laura had been so busy with all the new things in her life she hadn't had a chance to even think about a new project. Her fingers were itching to start something, and she'd been so pleased to discover there was actually a yarn shop in town.

Being an only child, she'd quickly discovered things she could do on her own. Reading had always been her way to try to make sense of the world around her, and after her mom's death, she'd lost herself in the pages of books, where she didn't have to deal with her own grief and her father's.

Before she went to high school, her maternal grandma, Laura, had taught her to knit and crochet. Since then, she'd never been bored. She'd never been one for crowds or parties and preferred listening to audiobooks while knitting or crocheting. It was a much more relaxing way to spend her time.

It also trumped dating. Seriously. Sitting in her jammies, not having to wear a bra, listening to a book, creating something with her hands—all way more fun than trying to stroke a man's ego just to make him feel good about himself. Not her job, she'd realized after only a few boring dates.

She'd also made an appointment to see the real estate agent today, so she'd pop into their offices when she was done with her shopping.

As she picked up her bag, her mind went back to Tuesday night's dinner at Arlene's. She still felt so uncomfortable that she'd asked about Walker. Goodness, she didn't know these people. She should've just listened. From everyone's reaction around the table, it had been clear it wasn't a subject the Westons liked to talk about.

Arlene's eyes had been bright with tears, Willow had tensed up, and the brothers had fallen silent. It was something that had happened five years ago, yet everyone was still in pain.

Sighing, she got out of her car. Every family had their secrets, their burdens. It's not as if she was getting involved with any of the Westons. When Luke moved to the next grade later this year, there would be no reason to mingle with them again.

Becket had texted and they were having dinner tonight at the Graff. She was looking forward to it. She liked him, and there were no strange vibes when she was with him. He was easy to talk to, so different from his grumpy brother.

Fortunately, she wouldn't have to see Grumpy anytime soon. Also, she could do with a good meal. There simply hadn't been time this week to buy or cook food. She'd ordered pizza one night and ate the leftovers the other night.

It was just after four, bitterly cold, and already nearly dark. Huddling in her coat, she looked at the shops on the other side of the street. Ooh, look—the lights were on inside the yarn shop. Delighted, she stepped into the road only to jump back quickly when a truck horn honked.

Lifting her hand to apologize to the driver, she quickly dropped it. Who'd be glaring at her through the front window? None other than Grumpy, of course. Ignoring him, she quickly crossed the road, exhaling when his truck drove away.

"Hello!" she called out as she opened the door of the yarn shop.

A beautiful blonde woman, more or less her own age, stood up from behind the one counter with knitting in her hand. A big smile lit up her face when she saw Laura. "Welcome, you're my first customer! I'm new to town and I've just opened the doors. I probably should've waited for tomorrow, but then I would've missed you." She held out her hand. "Eleanor Campbell, Ellie for friends."

Laura couldn't help smiling. She shook the woman's hand. "And I'm Laura Anderson. I've also just moved to Marietta."

"Then I want a hug!" Ellie smiled, and the next moment, her arms went around Laura and she was given a proper hug. "It's so good to meet another stranger. I was feeling a little bit lost among the townsfolk, who all seemed to know one another since forever. Are you looking for something specific? If I don't have it, I'll get it."

Laura laughed. "I am, actually. I'm a teacher at the elementary school and need another project for all the cold, winter evenings still ahead of us."

"Well, let me show you what new yarn I got in today…" She turned away and moved the box behind her to the side. "Books. I was a librarian for a long time." She smiled. "I have so many books."

"I don't believe one can ever have too many books," Laura said.

Ellie's face lit up. "A soulmate—how fabulous. I love books, always have. If you tell me your favorite author is George—"

"Eliot? Or rather, Mary Ann Evans?" Laura laughed.

Ellie gasped, then laughed. "Yes! I love, love *Middlemarch*, don't you? I try to read it every year. When re-reading books I've enjoyed when I was younger, I find a whole other book living under the one I thought I'd read. Oh, I hope we can have long talks about it? We can start a book club, we can sit and crochet or knit and talk books—what do you think? There is a space at the back we can use. After hours? What day? Who do we invite?"

Laura's head was spinning. Ellie's enthusiasm was infectious. "It sounds perfect. I'll ask around at school. I'm sure we'll find more people who like books and knitting…"

"Those are always the best people, don't you think?" Ellie handed Laura a business card." I got these today—what do you think of the name?"

"*ELLIE'S YARN COVE*," Laura read. "I love it." She turned around to look at the window. "It's on the window too—I missed it as I came in."

"How can you miss it?" Ellie cried out. "It's new and shiny and so pretty!"

Laura had to smile. "Sorry, I nearly had another unfortunate encounter with the bane of my existence since my arrival in Marietta."

"You mean"—Ellie dropped her voice—"Carol Bingley?"

Laura grinned. "I've only met her once. No, this was the dad of one of the kids in my class. But…" She glanced at her watch. "I have a date tonight and there are still several things I need to do, but I'll tell you all about it when we have our first book club-slash-knitting meeting. But now I need yarn. I was thinking of knitting a pretty, warm scarf—what can you recommend?"

"Over here." Ellie motioned and walked toward one of the big baskets in which an array of yarn was displayed. "Wow, you already have a date? You're a fast worker. How long have you been in town?" she teased as she pulled out the yarn.

"It's not really a date-date. He's just a friend. One of my neighbor's sons. Becket Weston."

Ellie's eyebrows rose. "Oh, him I've heard of."

"His own mother has warned me about him. Don't worry," Laura laughed. "Besides, I'm not looking for a relationship. I like dating, meeting new people, but I'm not interested in anything serious. I am, though, interested in the history of the town and the surrounding ranches, and Becket seems to know a lot about it. Once he understood I wasn't falling for his baby blues, he dropped the Casanova act. So, what about you? Any dates lined up?"

Ellie shuddered visibly. "No, thank you. Let's just say my experience with the opposite gender has put me off men for life. But—she grinned—"we are going to have so much fun with our book club. Text me, please? Then I'll have your number too."

Minutes later, Laura left the shop, her phone in hand and with much more yarn than she'd intended to buy. But how was a girl to choose from among all the pretty colors?

It was snowing lightly, and she covered her head with the hood of her parka. With a quick look to the right and then left, making sure the street was empty, she stepped off the curb while entering Ellie's phone number into her contacts.

The next moment, tires screeched, followed by an angry honk, and her heart just about leapt from her chest. Stunned, she stared at the truck that had come out of nowhere. A door slammed, and quick, irritated footsteps made their way over to her. Seriously, she didn't believe this. Grumpy. Again.

"I could've killed you!" he called out as he approached. Recognition dawned as he came closer. "You, again. What the hell are you doing standing in the middle of a street, texting?"

"You came out of nowhere," she huffed and turned away. "And I wasn't in the middle of the street."

A hand closed around her elbow. "Damn it, Laura, you could've been seriously injured," he growled.

Jerking her arm away, she stepped back, but one foot slipped. She was going to fall! Desperately, she looked for something else to grab on to except Hayden-freaking-Weston, but steel arms clamped around her before she could catch her breath and she ended up against Hayden's warm body again. Her hands on his chest. Again.

"Let me go!" she said through clenched teeth while trying to wiggle out of his arms.

"Damn it, woman, hold still." Taking her elbow in a firm grip, he walked her across the street.

Only when they'd safely reached the other side did he drop his hands. "That was the fourth time."

"What are you talking about?" She huffed out of breath, hitching her bag over her shoulder.

"You've touched me again," he said, his eyes narrowed. With a sigh, he rubbed his face. "Stay out of the damn street." Before she could respond, he walked away.

Exhaling slowly, she moved toward the bank on unsteady legs. Her whole body was tingling, her insides were a shuddering mess, and had it been her imagination or had she felt…? Shaking her head and muttering, she entered the bank. These ridiculous thoughts were only popping up because she'd ended up against Hayden Weston's body again.

Argh. She didn't have time for this…this craziness, damn it. She was on her way to talk to the bank manager to try to sort out her financial affairs. That was what she should be concentrating on, not the musky, earthy smell of a sexy cowboy.

The fourth time she'd touched him, he'd said. Why was he counting? And why was she still thinking about him?

A FAMILY WITH THE COWBOY

HAYDEN SAW BECKET'S text to the family chat group as he sat down to dinner.

Dining at the Graff with Laura tonight. Told Isabella so she wouldn't keep a plate for me

The swear word slipped out before Hayden could stop himself. What the hell was Becket doing with Luke's teacher? And why was it bothering him?

"People who swear don't have a vo… vo'bulary, Miss Anderson says," Luke said primly.

Her eyes dancing with mirth, Willow leaned forward. "Why are you using bad words, Hayden?"

"I just don't think what Becket is doing is a good idea."

"She's gorgeous." Cooper smiled. "If he hadn't made a move, I would've."

Hayden glared at his brother. "Since when do you date?"

"I date," Cooper said. "Sometimes."

"Well, why don't you and Hayden here go have a drink at the Graff tonight and make sure Becket behaves himself? Seeing you're both so interested in the teacher. I'll stay with my favorite nephew." Willow tousled Luke's hair.

"I didn't say—" Cooper began.

"Good idea. I'll pick you up in half an hour," Hayden heard himself interrupting.

Luke's head had been twisting this way and that as he

tried to follow the conversation around him. "Are you talking about my teacher?" he finally asked.

Hayden swallowed a groan. His son was nobody's fool.

"So, what would you like to do tonight, Luke?" Willow quickly asked. "What about—?"

"Can you read me a story?" Luke interrupted. "Miss Anderson says…"

While Luke went on and on about his teacher, Hayden ate his food, tasting nothing. He was ready to punch or kick something or someone. There wasn't time in a day to think about his needs, his feelings, damn it. He had a ranch to run and a son to raise.

So then why was he going to the Graff for drinks tonight?

Chapter Five

Laura finally relaxed. To be honest, she'd been worried they'd run into Becket's brothers tonight. It would be best for all concerned, she'd decided, if she didn't see more of the oldest Weston brother.

He bothered her. She didn't like the way she reacted to him. The strange vibes, the stupid butterflies in her tummy—she was twenty-nine, for goodness' sake. Who still got butterflies at nearly thirty?

Becket had ordered wine for them after asking her what she preferred to drink—she'd have to tell his mother she'd raised him well—and they'd just ordered food.

"So, why does a pretty lady like you decide to move to a small town like Marietta?" Becket asked with his big smile.

Laura laughed. "Don't waste those baby blues on me, okay? Your own mama warned me about you. Tell me about the history of your ranch."

"My moves are clearly wasted on you." Becket grinned.

"Clearly. Relax and tell me about your family history."

"Okay, if you're sure. You'll have to stop me, though. We're all very passionate about our land and once I start…"

"I'm sure. So shoot—when did the first Westons arrive here in Montana?"

"Okay, here goes. Way back, around the 1860s, there was a big demand for beef in the mining towns and that was when cattlemen appeared in the valleys around here…"

Becket had lost his flirty manner, and it was obvious he knew the history of the land around Marietta and particularly of their ranch. "The early ranchers relied on the practice of what is known as 'open range,' where they grazed large plots of unsettled lands, continually moving their herds to fresher pastures. I won't bore you with the details of all the problems the ranchers had back then. Then, at some point in the late 1800s and again in the early 1900s, there was legislation promising large parcels of land to applicants who would improve the land through agriculture. Many of the new ranchers also participated in the open range ranching, but the increase in fenced-in privatized land, plus the difficulty of managing livestock during cold winters, eventually led to the end of . . ."

A commotion behind them stopped Becket in the middle of his sentence. His eyes widened. "Damn it, I don't believe this," he muttered as he got up quickly. "Excuse me…"

"Becket," a woman cried. Laura turned her head to see a disheveled-looking blonde rushing toward Becket. "Why don't you answer my texts?" she cried out. "How can you be with someone…" she sobbed, pointing toward Laura, obviously distraught.

A FAMILY WITH THE COWBOY

With an apologetic backward glance in her direction, Becket steered the woman in the direction of the doors.

Ignoring all the glances in her direction, Laura took a sip of her wine. It was an awkward situation, but she was hungry and wasn't leaving before she finished her dinner. Hopefully, she'd be able to get an Uber.

Closing her eyes, she enjoyed the layers of baked cherry, blackberry, currant, and a hint of cardamom of the cabernet sauvignon Becket had ordered. No use wasting a lovely wine.

At the sound of scraping chairs, she opened her eyes. Hayden and Cooper Weston, both looking devastatingly handsome in neat pants and shirts, were sitting down at the table. Before she could get a word out, the waiter hastened closer.

"Another glass, please?" Cooper asked. "We've eaten, but we thought we could share your wine, if you don't mind, Laura?"

Hayden just stared at her.

"We're the rescue team," Cooper said as the waiter left. "Becket…um…has his hands full."

"Thanks." At least she sounded normal. "I don't really need rescuing at the moment. Maybe when I've finished my meal, I'd rather not walk home. And you're welcome to share the wine." She took out her phone and handed it to Cooper. "I was serious the other night when I said I want to get a dog. If you have one, that is. May I have your number?"

"Sure," Cooper said, entering his details. "Last week a

Jack Russell-kinda mutt turned up on my doorstep. She's clean now and got her shots, but she needs more attention than what I can give her. Might be hard to earn her trust. She hasn't had it easy, but you're welcome to come and have a look."

Laura smiled. "How do you know she had a tough time?"

Cooper shrugged. "She's told me."

Animal whisperer, Becket had called him. "I'll pop in sometime over a weekend, thanks. I'll let you know."

"What about tomorrow morning?"

Aware of the silent Hayden still staring at her, she glanced his way. "I still have some unpacking to do, but soon. I'll let you know."

"Sure, I'll send you directions to my house."

Hayden was glad Cooper was talking, because he was struggling to breathe, let alone talk. Barefoot, in jeans and a sweater, Laura was beautiful. All dressed up like she was tonight, she literally took his breath away.

In a soft pink top, cut low, leaving her shoulders bare, she had him just about salivating. Long golden earrings dangled from her ears, touching her neck every now and again as she moved her head. He couldn't stop staring at the exact points where they grazed soft skin every so often.

"...we regularly attend grazing workshops and talk about what the best practices are." Cooper's voice finally penetrated his befuddled mind. "...proper grazing techniques can improve overall land health. Our practices include high-density grazing with cattle herds, allowing adequate time for the soil to rest. It has led to some remarkable changes on our range lands." Cooper slapped Hayden on the shoulder. "But Hayden here is really the man to ask about that."

Just then, two waiters approached. One put the extra glass in front of Cooper and the other put one plate down in front of Laura. Hovering with the other plate in his hand, he looked at Hayden.

"Just put it down, thanks," Cooper said and waited for the waiter to leave before he spoke again. "Becket and Laura have been talking about grazing," he told Hayden, clearly amused. "Definitely a first for our Becket." He chuckled as he got up. "Excuse me, I see Aiden O'Sullivan and his wife over there. They were looking for a dog. By the way, Aiden has written a story on the deferred rotation system used around here. I'll send you the link if you're interested."

"Thanks, yes," Laura said, and Cooper walked away. "You really don't have to stay," she told Hayden, picking up her fork. "I'm fine eating alone. I often do."

"Damn it, Laura, I can't stop thinking about—" He stopped himself just in time before the "you" slipped out.

"Thinking about what?" she asked.

Staring at her mouth, he shook his head. What the hell

was happening to him?

Just then a harried-looking Becket returned. Frowning, he looked at Hayden. "What are you doing here?"

"Your date was sitting on her own."

He turned to Laura. "I'm so sorry, Laura, for leaving you alone, but it was the only way to avoid a total hysterical meltdown…"

Inhaling sharply, Laura put down her fork, picked up her bag, and got up. She'd had it with these Westons. "Please don't talk about women like that. Expressing one's feelings doesn't make you hysterical. It means you're human. You seem like a nice guy, Becket. Maybe if you let people see that, treat women with the respect they deserve, and stop trying to be the town Casanova, you won't need to deal with people you've hurt. Maybe you Weston boys should try talking about your feelings. I'm going home."

And turning on her heel, she walked away, head held high, leaving Hayden struggling to catch his breath. It was a good thing he hadn't known about the short black skirt and high heels she was wearing.

"She can't walk home in those heels," Becket said. "But I don't think she'll get into a car with me right now. You may have better luck, although I wouldn't bet on it." He grinned.

"Coop's with me…" Hayden began, just as Cooper returned.

"What's going on? Where's Laura?"

"Walking home in heels," Becket said.

Hayden got up. "I'll offer her a ride. You go with Becket," he said to Cooper.

"Who says I'm ready to go home?" Becket grinned.

Hayden glared at him. "I think you've given the folks here tonight enough to talk about for the next year. We have a business to run in case you've forgotten. You want respect? You need to earn it." He walked away, ignoring all the curious looks and whispers.

LAURA SLIPPED ON her coat as she quickly moved toward the exit of the hotel. The hotel had been restored over two and a half years ago, Becket had mentioned. The grand lobby glowed with lovely paneled wood, marble, and gleaming light fixtures, but she hardly noticed it again as she quickly made her way outside.

The only person she could blame for the fiasco of a date was herself. Hadn't she vowed to steer clear of men, of relationships? And here she was, not quite two weeks in a new town, and already in the middle of someone else's drama.

As she was digging into her purse for her phone, Aiden and Vivian O'Sullivan, Annie's sister and husband, who she'd met while staying at Annie's, stepped out of the hotel.

Frowning, Vivian walked up to her. "Everything okay, Laura?"

"We saw what happened inside. May we offer you a lift home?" Aiden asked.

"Thank you, yes. I'm so sorry…"

"We live on the same street. We're Arlene's neighbors on the other side," said Vivian, taking Laura's arm. "No problem."

Within minutes, the O'Sullivans dropped her off. Vivian walked with her to her front door. "Oh, my goodness, it's cold! We're from Portland, and I'm still not used to it." Vivian laughed. "I really admire the fact that you can walk in heels on these slippery surfaces."

"I'm from Missoula. It does get pretty cold there, too, so I'm used to it. But, yeah, heels aren't the best option in this weather."

"Will you be okay?" Vivian asked as Laura put the key in the front door.

"I'll be fine, thanks. I'm much happier at home, knitting and reading, than going on dates. I should remember that."

Vivian smiled. "Has nobody told you about the magic of this town? It has a way of opening up your heart, whether that's what you want or not."

"My heart is in no danger…"

Behind them was the crunch of tires on snow, and both Laura and Vivian turned around.

"You have a visitor," Vivian said, as Hayden got out of his truck. "You want us to hang around?"

Laura's heart was beating so loudly she barely heard Vivian's question. "It's okay. I'll be fine. He won't be staying. Probably just checking if I'm okay."

"Okay, we'll talk soon." With a wave, Vivian walked away.

Hayden had stopped to talk to Aiden, who was sitting in his truck, but as Vivian approached he nodded in her direction and walked toward Laura.

She unlocked the front door and switched on the light in the entrance hall, but didn't enter. If he had something to say, he could say it out here on the porch.

"I was going to bring you home," he said, as Aiden drove away.

"Not necessary. As you can see, I'm fine. Good night." As she quickly turned to open the door, her foot slipped. Everything happened in slow motion—her hand shot out to grab the doorknob, her bag dropped, her hand slid from the knob and two strong arms caught her before she could fall on the floor.

"Damn it to hell, woman," Hayden muttered as she fell against him. He staggered a few steps backwards through the open door into the house with her in his arms.

Out of breath, she lifted her head. His amber eyes turned darker and his jaw tightened. "You are touching me again," he growled, slipping his hands around her waist.

She should push him away, demand he leave, but something strange was happening. The whole entrance hall suddenly seemed to be vibrating with peculiar electric currents, and her limbs felt heavy. Moving was impossible.

Her senses took in everything: his strong jaw and wide, muscled shoulders, the earthy tones of his smell, his warm hands on her waist, the muscles moving beneath her fingers, his ragged breathing. Or was it hers?

"This time I'm going to respond," he murmured against her mouth, only millimeters separating their lips.

As if hypnotized, she stared at his mouth. She wanted this. His kiss. It was all she'd been thinking about since he'd knocked on her classroom door. Actually, no. She'd wanted this since she'd seen him in Grey's Saloon on her first night in Marietta.

But instead of kissing her mouth, his head dropped down and warm lips trailed over her shoulder, leaving feather-light kisses wherever they touched.

Before she could catch her breath, their lips met. Barely. She felt it down to her toes, though. Her breath hitched somewhere in her throat. Amber eyes roamed over her face once more before he took her mouth again.

This time a wild torrent simply picked her up, and all she could do was cling to him as one sensation after the other slammed into her. This was how one should be kissed. This was probably the kind of kiss Rhett Butler had been talking about when he'd told Scarlett O'Hara in *Gone with the Wind* she should be kissed often, and by someone who knew how. This guy…this guy was the Yoda of kissing.

She'd never experienced anything like this. This assault

on her senses, the merciless giving of pleasure until she was just about drowning in it—how was it possible that she hadn't known kissing could be like this?

Impatient hands were inside her coat, moving up and down her sides, igniting little fires under her skin as far as they went. She was burning up, her body moving restlessly against his, her only thought that he should never stop.

As the sound of a car honking nearby finally penetrated the fog in her brain, he lifted his head. His breath, like hers, was ragged, the amber pools darkened with desire.

"Hayden…"

With a soft swear word, he stepped back, rubbed his face. "I…I apologize. That…should never have happened. It's crazy. I…there is…I can't do this. I'm sorry."

Before she could utter a word, he walked out of the house. "Lock the door behind me," he called out as he pulled it close.

Still floating somewhere in space on a soft, pink cloud, her brain filled with lustful thoughts of warm hands on her body. What had just happened took another minute to sink in.

Hayden Weston had kissed her. Kissed her like she'd never been kissed before…wasn't there a song about it?

And then he'd left because it should never have happened.

After locking the door, she leaned her hot forehead against the cold surface of the wood. Her breath was still uneven, her heart racing at an alarming pace.

Inhaling deeply, she finally turned around and walked on alarmingly unsteady legs in the direction of her room. Like he'd said, it was crazy. He'd made it clear nothing could come of it, whatever "it" was and, anyway, hadn't she also vowed to steer clear of men?

In her room, she began pacing. This usually helped when she needed clarity on something.

The whole thing could be explained away if you looked at the facts: he'd been a widower for a while, she hadn't been with someone for…she couldn't even remember the last time she'd been kissed. And never by a real-life Rhett Butler, that was for sure.

For some reason or other, she'd ended up in his arms five times. Plus, they were both healthy adults, so feeling vibes between them wasn't that strange. What had happened between them was purely physical.

Calmer, she stopped pacing. There. She was going to forget it had ever happened and move on with her life. She had things to do—a house to buy, a scarf to knit, books to read.

Hours later, she was lying in bed, still wide awake, staring at the ceiling, reliving every single second of Hayden's kiss. With a groan, she turned on her side. Okay, it had happened only hours ago. She'd have to give it time. She'd forgotten all about the previous kisses she'd had. At some point, this one would also fade from her memory.

Closing her eyes, she willed herself to sleep.

Chapter Six

BY THE TIME Hayden returned to the homestead for breakfast on Saturday morning, he'd been up four hours. Turned out, if you really wanted to, there was a lot to do at four o'clock in the morning.

He couldn't sleep. Kissing Laura was all he could think about. She'd fitted perfectly in his arms and against his body. Even looking at another woman hadn't entered his mind over the past two years, let alone thinking of kissing one. Yes, he'd seen women around town, met women his friends had tried to set him up with, but it had been easy to smile and walk away.

And then, on an ordinary Friday night in Grey's Saloon, he'd looked up and seen Laura. Everything had changed in that moment. Since then, she'd invaded his dreams, his mind, his body.

He shouldn't have been in the Graff Hotel last night to begin with. And when he'd seen Laura was safely home, he should've driven away. But no, he had to get out of his car, walk up to her, and…he still wasn't quite sure how the kiss happened.

What the hell had he been thinking? Apart from anything else, she was his son's teacher, for heaven's sake. There wasn't time in the day to take a breath, let alone think about women or dating or sex. And now he couldn't stop thinking about any of it.

He had no business kissing strange women. He'd been married to the love of his life and he still missed Madeline. Love? Why was the word even popping up in his mind? Nobody was talking about love, damn it.

He hadn't had sex in a long time, and it was probably his body's way of reminding him of his needs. Besides, he probably was a decade older than she was.

Muttering at his own foolishness, he walked into the kitchen, where the rest of the family was having breakfast. Becket's dogs—Harper, a Labrador, and Jack and Sadie, two Golden Retrievers—got up and greeted Hayden as he entered.

"…and Miss Anderson says it's okay," Luke was saying, smiling, his eyes sparkling.

Willow laughed. "You like your new teacher, don't you?"

"Yes, she's very nice. And I like the books she reads to us." He looked down. "I'm not so sad all the time anymore."

Everyone around the table fell silent. Willow looked at him, widening her eyes. He should say something.

Dropping a hand on Luke's shoulder, Hayden cleared his throat. "Good to hear that, buddy." He sat down next to his son.

"Miss Anderson says Mom will always be in my heart. I like that." He looked at Hayden. "Can I read after my chores?" he asked.

"May I?" Willow corrected with a smile.

"May I, Dad?"

"I don't have a problem with you reading. But—"

"—chores come first." Luke nodded. "Miss Anderson says so too."

Hayden swallowed a groan. How the hell was he supposed to forget about the damn kiss if his son kept talking about Laura? "Don't you want to invite friends over, though?" he asked.

"Nah, I'd rather read. Miss Anderson says she also likes reading better than people." Hopping off his chair, he ran out of the kitchen, Jessie, as always, on his heels.

Willow laughed. "Well, rumor has it Miss Anderson seems to be keeping the Weston boys on their toes." She looked at the three of them. "Care to tell me what happened last night? I thought Becket was taking Laura for dinner. But from what I've heard, Becket had to stop Susanne from scratching out Laura's eyes. Then Hayden and Coop ended up at Laura's table. And, Hayden, there are unconfirmed rumors that you stopped Aiden's car in the middle of the street, grabbed Laura right out of it and took her home. Where you apparently—and there are numerous versions of this going around town—kissed her."

Cooper looked at his watch. "It's eight o'clock on a Saturday morning—where on earth have you heard all of that?"

Hayden was very much aware of Willow watching him, but he kept his eyes focused on his own plate. Ever since she was little, their sister had had the ability to read their minds. It used to freak them all out when they were younger. Still did, if he was honest. Especially in this particular moment, he'd rather not have anyone else know what was going on his mind.

"Well, as it turns out," Willow continued, "Betty from the police dispatch was having dinner in the Graff, and apparently, Carol Bingley was driving down Collier Road around the time Hayden stopped Aiden's car."

"I didn't stop his car," Hayden said. "Aiden and Vivian dropped Laura off. I went to Laura's house to make sure she was fine. It was all Becket's idea, by the way, not mine."

"And the rumor about the kiss?"

Hayden kept eating, studiously avoiding looking at his sister. "People should mind their own damn business."

Laughing, Becket slapped Hayden on the back. "It's about time you make the town gossip again, bro. I took Laura to dinner, Sis. We were having a very nice time talking about grazing…"

"Oh, really? Grazing?" Willow snickered.

"Really. She told me not to waste my baby blues on her." Becket grinned.

"Smart girl." Willow nodded.

"Anyway," Becket continued. "Susanne arrived at the

restaurant..."

Hayden tuned out his brother's voice and tried to eat. He was tired and angry and wanted to punch something. Without really tasting anything, he finished eating.

"Before you all leave"—Willow stopped him from getting up—"remember the Winter Ball next Saturday night. We've bought a table for eight people. I'm taking Mom as my date, so you boys need to get someone to go with you. And Becket, please make sure no previous girlfriends will rock up and ruin another night, will you?"

"I'm taking Luke," Hayden said quickly.

Willow laughed. "It's going to be interesting watching you trying to ignore Luke's beautiful teacher. You have a thing for her. I saw it on Tuesday night at Mother's already."

Hayden glared at her. "I don't know what you're talking about."

"You can't hide—" Willow began, but fortunately, Becket came to his rescue.

"I promise not to ruin the evening. Laura gave me an earful last night about my behavior." Becket smiled sheepishly. "Don't you start."

"Did she now?" Willow smiled. "I like her more and more." She pointed at Coop and Becket. "So, which one of you is going to ask her to the ball?"

Becket shook his head. "Something tells me the lady won't be overly eager to go with any of us."

Cooper got up. "She doesn't have a problem with me."

Hayden swallowed the "don't" that nearly slipped out.

Cooper's eyes met his. "Unless you have a problem with that?"

"Hayden?" Willow teased. "Do you have a problem with Coop taking Laura to the dance?"

Hayden turned away. "Why would I have a problem?"

"'Cause you kissed her?" Cooper said.

Ignoring them, Hayden walked toward the back door. "I'm in the barn." He needed something to kick or punch. Or both.

His family's laughter followed him all the way outside.

SATURDAY MORNING, JUST after ten, there was a knock on Laura's front door. She hadn't really slept last night. In between dreams of Hayden's warm hands all over her naked body, she'd been drinking water, trying to cool down. In the middle of winter.

She'd gotten up early and had just finished unpacking the last of the boxes. Her heart kicked against her ribs. It couldn't be Hayden, could it? Running on her socks to the door, she looked through the peephole. It was Arlene, his mother, thank goodness.

Combing her hair out of her face, she opened the door. "Arlene, it's so nice to see you. Everything okay?"

"That's what I came to ask you."

Laura blinked. "Yes, I'm fine. Why?"

"I've heard about last night. Everyone is talking about what happened at the Graff."

Laura opened and closed her mouth a few times before she opened the door wider. "Come on in. I'll make tea." In the kitchen, she switched on the kettle before she took out two cups and a teapot. "Let's sit here at the table. I've heard about the town gossip mill, but my goodness, it's only ten in the morning."

"Willow heard about it before eight. I thought you may be sleeping late."

"I was up early, still unpacking." She smiled as she made the tea.

"So you're fine?"

With her eyes on the teapot, Laura carried it to the table. "Becket and I are just friends. We were talking about the ranch when a woman approached him, crying. I don't like the way he treats women or talks about them and I've told him that…"

Arlene's eyes widened. "Good for you."

Laura continued as she poured the tea. "It was an awkward situation. Your two other sons tried to make it less so by joining me at the table. That was it."

"So when did Hayden kiss you?"

Laura just about choked on her tea and quickly put down her cup. "How on earth do you know that?" slipped out before she could stop herself.

Arlene's eyes were twinkling. "You have no idea how happy I am to hear Hayden is kissing again." Shaking her head, she sighed. "For the past two years, he's been walking around like a zombie. We were all still struggling with Walker's death when Madeline was diagnosed with breast cancer. Luke was only four. Hayden has always been the one who looked out for others. His biggest fear is that he won't be able to protect the ones he loves. And then both his brother and his wife died. He's erected such a hard shell around his heart, I've been worried nobody would be able to penetrate it. But something has changed over the last week. So what I want to know is, when are you seeing him again?"

Laura shook her head. "Apart from talking about Luke, there's no reason to."

"But what about the kiss?"

"You shouldn't believe everything you hear," Laura said, not meeting Arlene's eyes. At that moment her phone beeped. Glancing at it, she saw it was a text from Ellie. She wouldn't usually look at texts while talking to people, but she urgently needed to change the current topic of conversation.

Picking up her phone, she read the text and, thank goodness, without realizing it, Ellie had come to her rescue. "Oh great." She smiled, "I've wanted to ask you—do you knit or crochet, and do you like books?"

Arlene blinked. "Yes, to all three, but..."

Putting down her phone, Laura leaned back in her chair.

For the moment, she wouldn't have to talk about kissing Hayden. "A new yarn shop has just opened in town. Did you know? I've met the owner, Ellie Campbell. We've just clicked. She's one of those people you can't help but like. We've talked about starting a book club in her shop where we'll knit or crochet and talk about books. That text was from her—the first meeting of the book club is Tuesday at six. You're welcome to join us, if you're interested?"

"That sounds wonderful. Since I moved to town, I have more time on my hands. Have you decided which book you want to discuss?"

For the next half hour, they talked books and knitting. When Arlene got up to leave, Laura escorted her to the front door. She was just about to close the door behind Arlene when the older woman turned around. "Come for lunch tomorrow? I'm making my famous chicken."

Laura hesitated. Would the rest of the family be there? "I…um…".

Arlene's eyes were twinkling. "I promise not to talk about Hayden kissing you. See you at twelve!"

Laura closed the front door. She should've said no. Arlene was the mother of the guy who had kissed her senseless, and the older woman was bent on getting answers one way or the other.

Books, she remembered, relieved, seconds later. They'd talk about books. She'd managed to sidetrack Arlene once; she could do it again.

Chapter Seven

IT WAS JUST before one on Sunday when Hayden stopped in front of his mom's house. His siblings had arrived before him in Cooper's truck and were already walking toward the front door.

As he got out of his truck, he glanced toward Laura's house. He needed to talk to her, apologize again, and make sure she knew the kiss hadn't meant anything.

Yeah, right. If it hadn't meant anything, why was the lingering warmth of the vibrant floral scent surrounding her still with him? Why couldn't he stop thinking about the softness of her mouth, the silkiness of her skin, the way her hair fell straight down to her shoulders…?

"Hayden?" Willow called out. "I have an idea in the next few minutes you're going to be pleasantly surprised, whether you want to or not. Come on."

Muttering under his breath, Hayden moved toward them. Luke had already joined his aunt and uncles on the porch of his mom's house while he was still staring at Laura's house.

Willow had an uncanny way of just knowing what was

going to happen, but it was Sunday lunch at his mom's. His mom was a great cook, so there would be no surprise there.

The front door opened, his mom appeared, and she opened her arms when Luke rushed forward. "Do I have a surprise for you, young man!" she said hugging him.

"What?" Luke asked.

"Not what, who?" His mom smiled, motioning for them to enter.

Hayden frowned. What was his mother talking about?

"This is going to be an interesting lunch." Willow chuckled as she followed their mother into the house.

"Come on. We're still pottering around in the kitchen. Hayden, will you open a bottle of wine for us? I like a sauvignon blanc with chicken, but open whatever else you guys like. There is also beer in the fridge, Cooper. And then you can tell me all about misbehaving in the Graff Hotel, Becket."

"What have you heard?" Becket asked, shaking his head.

His mother turned and looked straight at Hayden. "Oh, everything."

"She knows about the kiss too," Willow whispered loudly to Hayden behind her hand.

"What kiss?" Luke asked as they all entered the kitchen.

"The one your dad gave—"

"Mom!" Hayden cut her short.

Her eyes brimming with mirth, she winked at him. "He's going to hear about it eventually. You may as well tell him.

Say hello to Laura!"

He looked up and there she was—looking so beautiful, his chest hurt. In a blue top the color of fields of lavender, a pair of jeans hugging her slender body in all the right places, she took his breath away.

Flustered, she put down the plates she'd been carrying. "Oh, Arlene, you should've told me it's a family lunch…" she said, avoiding his eyes.

"Miss Anderson!" Luke cried out, obviously happy to see his teacher. He rushed forward and hugged her legs.

Smiling, Laura crouched down in front of him. "It's so nice to see you," she said, combing his hair from his face.

Hayden's heart tightened at the sight of his son with his teacher. Luke was grinning from ear to ear, clearly happy just to be near her.

As Laura got up, Willow took her arm. "You're mom's neighbor and friend. That makes you also family. On Sundays we eat in the dining room. Come and sit with me while the boys get us wine. Tell me about the knitting-crochet-book club idea my mother can't stop talking about." And with a wink in Hayden's direction, Willow steered Laura out of the kitchen.

WITH HER HEAD reeling, Laura tried her best to focus on what Willow was saying, but she only managed to catch a word here and there. Although she hadn't been ready to see Hayden again, her body was very happy. The butterflies in her tummy were going berserk, her hands were clammy, her heart was doing joyous cartwheels, her breasts…oh, my goodness, her breasts were tingling in anticipation.

How was she going to survive the lunch if the mere sight of him rendered her just about speechless?

"You feel something for him?" Willow's soft words penetrated her wild thoughts.

Fortunately, at that point, the others returned. Quickly, she jumped up. "I should help Arlene…"

"Everything is here," Arlene called out.

Luke grabbed her hand. "Grandma says I can sit next to you!" He grinned as he led her to the table.

Focusing on Luke, she only realized Hayden was sitting on her other side once she'd sat down. He was so close she could feel the heat radiating from his body. She inhaled shakily. Big mistake. Tones of his musky, earthy scent filled her lungs. Help.

"What can I get you, Laura?" Cooper asked. "Sauvignon blanc or a merlot? Both wines are from wineries in West Montana. You may know them?" he asked as he held one of the bottles for her to look at.

Unable to focus on anything, she smiled and nodded. "Anything, thanks."

"Give her some of the sauvignon blanc, Coop." Arlene smiled. "I think you'll like it, Laura. So, how are you settling in?"

"It will take a while, but I love the house."

"I've heard Lydia Gearing wants to sell, so I hope it doesn't happen too quickly," Arlene smiled.

"Well…" Laura hesitated. She wasn't used to discussing her business with people she hardly knew, but as she'd discovered yesterday, everyone did indeed know everything in this small town. "I've put in an offer to buy the house. I'm hoping to hear by Monday."

"What splendid news!" Arlene smiled. "I'm so happy for you. You're going to love living here. There is always something going on. Next weekend, for instance, is the Winter Ball…"

"You remember you're my date, Mom?" Willow said.

"Yes, thanks, Willow, but won't you rather—?"

"No, Mom," she interrupted quickly. "I won't."

"What about you boys?" she asked her sons.

"Luke is my date," Hayden said.

"I'm going on my own," Becket grinned.

"I was wondering if you'd like to go with me, Laura?" Cooper asked.

Next to her, Hayden stiffened.

"I was going to text you…" Cooper smiled.

"Winter Ball?" she repeated, stalling, trying to think what to say. She liked Cooper. That wasn't the problem. The problem was sitting right next to her—he was also going to be there.

"Yes." Arlene nodded. "Everyone dresses up. There is a live band…"

"Mom." Becket laughed. "Maybe you should explain the 'band' are people with other jobs who just like to make music together every now and again."

"The last time I've been to a dance was as a student. I don't—" Laura said.

"Everyone will be there," Arlene interrupted.

"I don't have anything to wear…" Laura tried again.

"Great," said Arlene. "That means we can go shopping. Willow, what do you say? If we leave for Bozeman on Saturday morning early, we can be back before lunch."

"Ooh, that sounds fabulous." Willow grinned.

Cooper smiled. "If you don't wanna go…"

"I'd love to go, thanks," she heard herself saying. "What time Saturday morning?" she asked Arlene.

BY THE TIME Hayden got home, he was ready to punch his brother. The fact that Luke had been talking nonstop about his teacher during the drive home didn't help, either.

Normally Cooper was the quiet one, the one who listened rather than talked. That hadn't happened today. No, today he'd talked and flirted with Laura and made jokes, so unlike his usual self even Luke had asked him at some point if he was feeling okay.

As he and Luke walked toward the house, Cooper's truck stopped behind them. Luke was racing toward an ecstatic Jessie.

"Is there a problem?" Hayden asked, irritated by his siblings' grinning faces.

"If you have a thing for Laura, do something about it." Coop grinned. "Don't keep glaring at me."

"I'm amazed he hadn't slugged you." Becket laughed. "There were several moments when he looked ready to put his fist in your face."

"I don't have a damn 'thing' for anyone," Hayden growled.

Of course, Willow also had to chip in. "Oh, really? You can't take your eyes off of her, yet you kept staring daggers at poor Cooper here, who only tried to keep the conversation going, seeing that you weren't saying anything."

"I'm happy to take Luke to the dance if you wanna swap dates," Cooper teased.

With a short expletive, Hayden stomped away. He'd had it with his siblings, with this day, with all these crazy, unwanted feelings swirling inside of him, making him aware that he was a man, that he had needs.

Inside the house, he leaned against the first wall, trying to control his breathing. Yes, Laura was gorgeous. He noticed, but he couldn't do anything about it, could he? Just for a moment, the possibility that he could phone Laura, that he could make a date with her, find out whether this craziness was something real, had his heart racing.

Damn it. He pushed away from the wall. How could he even think about a second chance at happiness? He didn't deserve it, damn it. Walker hadn't even had one chance to be happy, to fall in love, to raise a family. He'd died way too young. And he, Hayden, was to blame.

So it didn't matter that he wanted Laura with every breath he took—he was ready to admit that to himself, at least—he could never do anything about it. Besides, it was probably lust, pure and simple. This craziness would disappear at some point. It had to.

"Dad?" Luke asked behind him and a small hand slipped into his.

Crouching down to look his son in the eye, the way he'd seen Laura do, he smiled. "Would you like some ice cream? And then I'd like it if you read something to me from one of your books."

Luke's eyes widened. "Do you have time for that?" he whispered.

Hayden swallowed. He hadn't realized it before now, but he was always telling Luke he was busy, he didn't have time. It was easier to avoid spending time with his son, who looked so much like his mom, than think about the pain of losing Madeline. "I'm making time." Hayden grinned and, in one move, he got up and, swooping Luke up in his arms, he put him on his shoulders.

With Luke shrieking with delight and Jessie barking

around their feet, Hayden walked toward the kitchen. "Let's see what kind of ice cream Isabella has for us in the fridge."

He had a son to look after. There was no time for lusting after a gorgeous blonde with blue eyes and soft skin and the most kissable mouth…

Damn, this wasn't helping.

Chapter Eight

TUESDAY NIGHT IN Ellie's Yarn Cove was a loud and lively affair. Annie, her sister, Vivian, their sister-in-law, Riley, and the O'Sullivans' aunt, Janice, were all there. And Maria, Laura's colleague from school, also showed up.

When Laura had picked up Arlene, a smiling Willow also got into her car. Turned out, Annie had wandered into the yarn shop the previous day, heard about the book club, and brought the women in her family along.

Apart from a soft, "I've heard about Saturday night," Ellie hadn't mentioned Laura's date with Becket again.

In between gossiping and talking about yarn, they talked about possible books they'd want to discuss. Jane Austen's books were mentioned and Ellie, who seemed to know everything about all things Austen, gave them some interesting background detail. *Pride and Prejudice* would be the first book they'd discuss. *Middlemarch* would be a project for later in the year.

"Oh, I love this!" Ellie said as they all got up at the end of the evening. "I've so enjoyed tonight."

"I can talk books all day long. Since I've discovered audiobooks, I can bake and listen to stories at the same time," Annie added with a grin.

"Thanks for all the interesting background information, Ellie," Vivian said, and they packed up their knitting and moved toward the door. "I, for one, am happy I wasn't born during the late 1700s. I can't imagine not having the freedom to choose whom I want to marry or what I want to do with my life."

"Getting married was just about the only option for women back then," Janice added. "Not because you loved someone, but because your father or brother decided it for you. I'm very glad that has changed."

Ellie grinned, opening the door. "I'm happy that I have the choice to not get married. After my last relationship..." She visibly shuddered. "Let's just say I prefer being on my own."

"See, Mom?" Willow laughed. "I'm not the only one who isn't interested in love and marriage."

"Until the right person comes along." Annie laughed. "I'm telling you, there is something about this town..."

"I've warned Laura," Vivian said.

"Don't make the same mistake I did," Janice said. "Don't let love pass you by. Life is so very short. Will we see all of you at the Winter ball?"

"Yes, we're all going," Arlene said. "Cooper is taking Laura."

Ellie frowned. "Cooper? But didn't you go on a date

with…Becket, was it?"

"And she kissed Hayden." Willow grinned.

Maria smiled. "I've been trying to get more details out of her at school about the kissing everyone is talking about, but she just clams up."

Janice's eyes were twinkling as she looked at Laura. "Oh, I'm so glad to hear that. I love hearing about romance and kissing."

"No romance. We are all just friends," Laura said quickly. "Are you going to the dance, Ellie?" Time to change the topic.

Groaning, Ellie shook her head. "Oh, please, no! I can't think of a worse way to spend an evening. I have a new book and new yarn—so I have everything that makes me happy."

Janice gave Ellie a hug. "I can predict that, sooner or later, you're going to lose your heart to someone in Marietta. I do believe in the magic of Copper Mountain."

Riley groaned. "Seriously, Aunt Janice, I thought you were done with matchmaking."

"I'm just saying," Janice said innocently.

Vivian took her arm. "Yeah, right. Let's get you home before you start meddling in other people's lives."

Laughing, they all left.

Driving back to drop off Willow and her mother, Laura was quiet, thinking of Janice's words: Don't let love pass you by.

"…feel about marriage, Laura?" Willow's voice finally

penetrated her thoughts as she stopped in front of Arlene's house.

Laura shook her head. "I'm not relationship material, I've been told. And I think so too. I was raised by my dad. Mom passed away when I was eight. So I'm used to doing things on my own. The freedom to choose my own path, to be independent, is important to me, and I don't know if I'm willing to give that up. I'm really happy on my own, happy to be single. Men can be so exhausting, don't you think?"

"See, Mom?" Willow grinned. "More women feel that way. Fortunately, we don't have to get married in this day and age."

Arlene groaned. "Don't give Willow more ideas, Laura. You don't have to lose your independence when you marry, you know? When you meet the right guy, he will love the fact that you can stand on your own two feet."

"I have just moved to a new town, got a new job, and I'm buying a house—I think I have enough to keep me busy," Laura said.

Arlene and Willow got out of the car.

"Keep an open mind, that's all I'm saying," Arlene called out.

"Sorry about Mom. She's a romantic. Thanks for the lift," Willow said. "I'll pick the two of you up on Saturday morning."

"I don't know about the dance—" Laura tried, but Willow interrupted her.

"It's going to be fun," Willow smiled. "It always is."

FRIDAY AFTER SCHOOL, Hayden knocked on Laura's classroom door, his hat in his hand. He'd asked a friend to keep an eye on Luke while he talked to the teacher. He'd rather not go to her house to do it. This way, his mother wouldn't see him.

The door opened. His breath left his body in one swoosh. She looked incredible.

"Hayden?" she asked. "Is Luke okay?"

"Luke's fine. May I come in?"

"Yes, of course." She stood to the side to let him in. "Was there something about Luke you wanted to discuss?"

He shook his head. "He's changed so much since you became his teacher. Thank you for that. His mom's passing—it was hard on both of us."

"Of course it was. It will always be. I lost my mom when I was eight and I still miss her every day. Time makes it easier, though."

He nodded. "I also wanted to apologize for last Saturday night."

"Apologize for what?" she asked.

Damn, this was harder than he'd thought. But he had to get this out. "For grabbing you and…and kissing you."

She lifted an eyebrow. "From what I remember, you

didn't grab me. You told me you were responding to my touching you again. You gave me plenty of time to push you away, but I didn't. We kissed, Hayden. It's no big deal." She turned away. "I'll probably kiss a number of guys in and around Marietta before long."

Whether it had been his intention all along, or whether it was the roaring in his head, or the way she'd lifted her chin, he would never know, but the next moment, he'd thrown his hat down and was pulling her closer. "So kissing me is no big deal? Let's test that theory," he challenged as he combed a strand of hair from her face. "It's all I've been thinking about since last Saturday, all I've been dreaming about. And then I had to sit next to you on Sunday, feel you next to me, just to hear you agreeing to go to the dance with my brother? And you want to tell me kissing me is no big deal? Maybe you're right, maybe I've imagined what happened between us. Let make sure, shall we?"

The last words, he murmured against her lips. He waited another second, giving her time to say no or push him away, before he kissed her. Her mouth was soft and sweet and welcoming—just the way he remembered.

Only when she melted against him did he lift his head. "You feel what you do to me? And I can feel your reaction to me," he said, deliberately brushing the back of his hand against her straining nipples. Her breath hitched and her eyes darkened. "If anyone else you kiss makes you feel like this, I'll agree us kissing isn't a big deal," he said before he turned on his heel and strode out of the classroom.

Rubbing his face he walked as quickly as he could. What the hell? The idea had been to apologize to her, not kiss her again. Inhaling deeply, he leaned against his truck. He could still taste her on his mouth.

"Dad?" Luke asked as he ran closer. "You okay?"

"Of course, let's go." They got into the truck.

"Have you seen Miss Anderson?" Luke asked. And after a beat, "She's pretty, isn't she?"

Hayden quickly glanced at his son. There was a knowing glint in his little boy's eyes he'd never seen before. "Yeah, son. She's pretty." He smiled. Too damn pretty for his peace of mind.

He had to put Laura Anderson out of his mind and stay away from her. That was the only way he was going to get the pretty teacher out of his mind and dreams.

WILLOW PICKED LAURA up just after eight on Saturday morning, so by the time the shops opened in Bozeman, they were entering a mall.

Laura trailed behind Willow and Arlene. Coffee. She needed coffee. She hadn't slept a wink last night. Every time she'd drifted off, there was Hayden, his hot mouth on hers, his lower body throbbing against hers. Oh, my goodness, that was so not something to be thinking about when she was with his mom and sister.

"Let's try this store," Arlene was saying as she motioned toward a boutique. "I usually get what I'm looking for here. Do you have something specific in mind, Laura?"

"I was thinking a little black dress." Laura smiled, admiring the beautiful clothes in the shop. "Something I can wear again."

"Surely we can do better than that!" Arlene exclaimed. "Oh, Willow, look at this gorgeous skirt!" she exclaimed as she took a skirt from the rail.

As Laura turned to walk to one of the other racks, she saw a dress hanging against a cupboard. In the palest of blues, the bodice of the classic A-line dress was cut in such a way that it would leave her shoulders bare. It was beautiful.

Before she even touched the dress, she knew this was the one she was going to buy. Because she could already see Hayden's eyes darkening, could feel his warm lips on her shoulder…

"It's a beautiful dress," Arlene said behind her. "Are you going to try it on?"

"Ooh, and look at these heels," Willow exclaimed as she rushed closer, a pair of silver heels in her hand.

"I don't know…"

"Just try it on. We've found something to try on as well. This is so nice!" Arlene was all smiles as they walked toward the changing rooms. "We haven't done this in a while."

In the small changing room, Laura slipped out of her

own clothes and tried on the dress. It was a perfect fit. So were the heels.

Logic started asking all sorts of questions: was this really the best idea? She was his son's teacher, he was a widower, and surely the whole thing had heartache written all over it? She didn't even know the man. But he'd kissed her again, her heart reminded her. And he'd told her he'd been dreaming about her. And those amber eyes had a way of looking right into her soul…

Her heart won. Of course. She quickly got out of the dress and put on her own clothes again. She was going to regret this at some point, but right now, she was following Janice's advice—give love a chance.

Her breath hitched. Love? Nobody was talking about love. Hayden was an attractive man, a cowboy to boot, and he knew how to kiss. That was all. Besides, she was going to the ball with his brother. And maybe Hayden had changed his mind and was bringing another date besides his son to the ball.

She liked pretty clothes, and she hadn't bought something new for herself in a long while. This dress was for her, not for anyone else.

Yeah, right. Logic had the last say.

Chapter Nine

BY THE TIME Laura followed Cooper into the Graff Hotel, where the Winter Ball was being held, she was still berating herself for agreeing to his invitation. He wasn't the problem, of course. Dressed in black jeans, a white shirt, and a jacket, he looked very handsome.

She liked him. He was nice. He was easy to talk to. Not one of her body parts misbehaved around him, and there were absolutely no sparks driving her crazy. But… within the next few minutes, she was going to see Hayden too.

Just thinking about him woke up the butterflies in her tummy.

"I can see Willow's head," Cooper said as he motioned toward the opposite door. "Our table is over there."

As they passed other tables, they were greeted by other guests already sitting at tables. Most people who nodded and smiled in her direction were parents of the kids she was teaching. She hadn't been here very long, but she already knew a few people.

"Miss Anderson, Miss Anderson!" several voices suddenly cried out, and three of the girls in her class rushed closer.

"You look so pretty, Miss Anderson!" Becky Taylor smiled shyly.

Birdie Abbott touched her dress with reverence. "I like your dress, Miss Anderson."

"And I like your shoes," added Lucy Jones, who had been staring at Laura's shoes.

Laura crouched down and smiled at them. "Are you enjoying yourselves?"

They were so excited, they all started talking at once. Laura listened and nodded and smiled until Birdie's mom called them back to their table. Waving at Birdie's mother, Laura followed Cooper, who had been waiting patiently.

"Sorry about that."

"They obviously adore you." He smiled as he put a hand to her back and steered her toward the table where the rest of his family were already sitting. "I have to say, my second-grade teacher looked very different than you do."

Cooper's words faded as Laura caught Hayden's gaze on her. Both he and Becket got up as they neared the table. Becket was smiling, but Hayden's teeth were tightly clenched, his eyes shuttered, not giving anything away.

The butterflies in her tummy went ballistic. Her heart just about jumped out of her chest, and the roaring in her ears drowned out every other noise. Becket's mouth moved, but she had no idea what he said, as she smiled and nodded to him and to Arlene and Willow.

Without his hat, in black jeans and a black shirt, Hayden

was mouthwateringly sexy. Only when a small hand slipped into hers was she able to drag her eyes away from the gorgeous cowboy on the other side of the table.

"Hi, Luke," she said. "Don't you look handsome!"

"Grandma got me new clothes." He smiled proudly. "Where are you going to sit?"

"She's sitting next to me, buddy." Cooper grinned. "But I'm sure if you ask nicely, she'll save you a dance."

"Will you, Miss Anderson?"

Gravely, Laura nodded. "It would be my honor, thank you."

Happy, Luke skipped away.

Cooper pulled out a chair for Laura next to Willow and, gratefully, she sat down. At least she'd be able to talk to Willow and Arlene while trying not to stare at Hayden.

"Laura, okay if I get us a bottle of wine?" asked Cooper, who was still standing.

"Thank you, yes. And water, please?"

"Will do." He smiled as he turned away.

"You look lovely." Willow said.

"Thanks. So do you. And Arlene, I love that color on you."

"Thank you, my dear," Arlene said. "It's a pity your friend Ellie didn't want to come tonight. She could've met a lot of potential customers."

"Who's Ellie?" Becket asked.

"A new woman in town," his mom laughed when Becket

sat up straight. "Don't even think about it. She's so not the type of woman you'll like," his mother said quickly, winking at Willow. "She actually has a brain. And a sharp one, from what I've seen."

Luke tugged on his grandma's arm and she bent down to listen to him.

"She's just opened up a yarn shop in town," Willow said. "Next to the pharmacy. But as Mom said, not your type. She's started a book club."

Becket shuddered visibly. "You're right. Yarn and books—so not my type."

Just then a drumroll announced the band was ready. Becket jumped up. "Come on, Sis. Let's dance."

As they walked away, Luke appeared at Laura's side, holding out his hand. "May I have this dance?" Looking over his shoulder toward his grandma, he grinned. "Like that, Grandma?"

Arlene laughed. "Exactly like that, Luke. You could teach certain other people around the table how it's done."

HAYDEN WAS GNASHING his teeth as he watched his son walk toward the dance floor with Laura. How he was going to survive this night, he had no idea.

Laura looked gorgeous. His eyes had zoomed in on her milk-white shoulders the moment he'd seen her. His first instinct was to jump up, throw her over his shoulder, and take her home, where nobody but him could look at her.

Where did that come from? She was his son's teacher. That was all. This madness that had taken hold of him whenever she was around…he simply had to ignore it until it went away. He needed to stay as far away from her as possible until he could see straight again.

Cooper returned from the bar with two bottles of wine and water for Laura. Glancing toward the dance floor, he smiled. "I see Luke has stolen my date."

"You'd better go and stake your claim," Arlene said. "Luke isn't the only one who wants to dance with her."

Hayden turned to see a man approaching Laura and Luke. He recognized the cowboy as Dan Smith, an employee on Higgins Valley, a neighboring ranch.

Tipping his head, he swallowed a big gulp of his beer. Damn it, he didn't want to watch Laura dancing with someone else. But…she was free to dance with anyone she wanted to. It had nothing to do with him.

"Well, she's not exchanging partners," his mother said. "Good for her."

His head turned in her Laura's direction again. The cowboy was walking away, scowling, and Laura was laughing down at Luke. His heart settled down.

Only when the song ended did Laura and a beaming Luke return to the table.

"Hayden-freaking-Weston," someone said from behind

Hayden.

Hayden turned around to see who was talking before he got up slowly. From the corner of his eye, he saw Cooper moving closer.

It was Tim Higgins, the owner of Higgins Valley. After Hayden and his brothers had begun with the practice of high-density grazing on the Weston Ranch and had proof to show the way it improved the land, Hayden had invited the owners of neighboring ranches to come look at what they'd done. They had to work together to preserve the land for the next generation was his argument, and they'd tried to persuade the other ranchers to also give the system a try.

Many ranchers had been impressed with what they'd seen and had been happy to try out the new system. And when they got similar results to that on the Weston Ranch, even more ranchers tried it. Tim, however, was one of a few ranchers who hadn't been interested in changing anything.

Tim wasn't steady on his feet. If the rumors were true, they were having a difficult winter.

"Tim." Hayden nodded.

"You..." Tim said and pushed a finger into Hayden's shoulder. "You're the reason we..." He staggered backward.

Hayden looked at Cooper. "Maybe we should take this outside..."

Coop's eyes widened. "Watch out—" but before Hayden could ask what for, a punch landed on his face. It wasn't hard and mostly missed him, but he tasted blood in his mouth, nevertheless.

"Tim!" A clearly distraught woman rushed closer. Tim's wife, Sheryl. She tried to grab her husband's arm, but he pulled away, stumbled, and swore. "I'm so sorry, Hayden, I don't know what came over him," his wife said, her eyes filled with tears.

Becket appeared and put his hand on Tim's shoulder. "Let me buy you a nice, strong coffee, Tim," he said.

Tim tried to shake him off, but Cooper put a hand on his other shoulder, and together, he and Becket steered Tim toward the door, his wife hurrying after them.

Muttering under his breath, Hayden touched his face and looked around. There was no sign of Laura or Luke. Some people were looking curiously in their direction, but the music was loud enough that most of the guests seemed not to have noticed what had happened.

"Where's Luke?" he asked.

Willow motioned toward the dance floor. "Laura quickly led him back to the dance floor when Tim appeared."

And there she was, dancing with his son, trying to distract him.

"You're bleeding," his mom said. "Let me…"

"I'm fine. Excuse me."

***

LAURA JOKED AND teased Luke until his smiled returned.

She'd managed to get him back on the dance floor before his father was hit. Her insides were still shaking. The moment she'd seen the man behind Hayden, she knew something was wrong and she should get Luke away from the table as soon as possible. While she was steering him back to the dance floor, she'd caught a glimpse over her shoulder of the man punching Hayden. She couldn't believe what had happened, but she had to try to prevent Luke from seeing what was going on.

"I think I need a sip of water." She smiled as walked toward the table with Luke.

As they neared, Arlene motioned to Luke, and he ran toward his grandma.

"Thank you," Willow said softly.

"Hayden okay?" Laura asked.

"I think so. He's excused himself. He was bleeding."

"Bleeding?" Laura felt ill.

"Just—" Willow began, but Laura was already moving away.

She had to make sure he was okay.

As she walked through the doors, Hayden came out of the bathroom, touching his face. She stopped, her heart settling back in place. He didn't seem badly injured.

He looked up, dropped his hand, and walked over to her. "Where's Luke?"

"With your mom. You okay?"

He nodded, his gaze roaming her face. "You look beautiful."

"Thank you. You..." But tears clogged up her throat and she couldn't speak. "Excuse me," she muttered and hastened toward the ladies' room. What was wrong with her? Hayden was fine, she was fine. Everyone was fine.

Except... Fortunately, the bathroom was empty for the moment. She looked in the mirror while rinsing her hands. Nothing was fine. Nothing would ever be fine again. Because...Hayden. She'd kissed him, he'd touched her, and all she could think about was being with him.

Groaning, she dropped her head. She'd moved to another town to start afresh with the distinct goal not to get entangled with a man. Every single experience she'd had with the opposite sex had left a bad taste in her mouth, but what had happened? The very first cowboy she'd laid eyes on had her just about hyperventilating and ready to jump into his arms.

Seriously, she had to stay away from Hayden Weston.

Chapter Ten

HAYDEN STRODE BACK into the big hall. He shouldn't have come tonight. Hadn't he told himself to stay away from Laura? To forget about her? But here he was when he knew she'd be with his brother.

His mom was the only one sitting at their table. Luke and a friend were playing close by. He'd wait for Willow or Coop to return to sit with their mom before he and Luke went home.

"You okay?" his mom asked.

Pulling out a chair, he nodded. "Luke and I will be leaving shortly. Where's Willow?"

"Dancing with Hunter Grant." She chuckled. "I'm not sure how he got her on the dance floor. She was adamant about not dancing, but there they are..." She motioned toward the floor.

Hayden saw his sister dancing with Hunter. The cowboy had been working on the Circle C, one of the big ranches outside Marietta. He was a hard worker, didn't talk too much, and knew his way around a ranch.

"Rumor has it Hunter has a ranch waiting for him in

Colorado," his mother continued. "I like him. He can handle our Willow."

"Mother, please don't try and play matchmaker, will you? None of us are interested in a relationship. We're all still…" He swallowed the rest of his sentence. He never spoke about Walker's death if he could help it. Why would it slip out while he was at a dance?

His mother put a hand on his arm. "Grieving? I know, son. So am I. You've lost a brother and a wife. But life goes on and so should all of you. You can all keep blaming yourselves for an accident that happened five years ago or you can decide to live life."

"It's not that easy."

"Nothing worthwhile ever is, my dear," she said. "You like Laura. Everyone can see that. Why do you think Coop invited her here tonight? He was hoping to make you jealous. So do something about it."

"I'm still mourning my wife, damn it, Mom."

"It's been two years. She'd want to see you happy. We all would."

"I've been married and we were happy. I have Luke to look after. There isn't time for anything else."

"Oh, nonsense, Hayden. You're thirty-eight. You still have your whole life ahead of you. You want to spend all that time alone?"

Hayden was saved by the band. The members had taken a short break, but they were back behind their instruments and the first notes of a song filled the air.

"Listen to the song... *And then he kissed her.*" His mom smiled. "An old favorite. Here comes Laura. Loosen those reins you're holding on to so tightly and ask her to dance with you."

He looked, spotting her immediately among the crowd. Somehow, he always knew where she was. As he watched, three little girls stopped her. Smiling, she crouched down to talk to them for a few minutes before she got up, hugged each one in turn, and made her way over to the table.

She smiled vaguely in his direction, but didn't meet his eyes. "They're so sweet," she was saying to his mother as she sat down.

He was standing next to her chair, holding out his hand to her without having intentionally decided to do that. "Dance with me?"

Surprised, she looked up and opened her mouth to say something, but instead, she put her hand in his and got up. Without taking his eyes off her, he led her to the dance floor.

And then she was in his arms, her hand lying on his shoulder. He pulled her close and they began to move. Effortlessly, they glided over the floor. He was no dancer, but somehow Laura had quickly adjusted to his rhythm.

The song was all about kissing. Dropping his head he trailed his lips over a petal-soft, naked shoulder. It had been driving him crazy ever since he'd seen her as she'd entered. Like satin. Hot, so hot.

Inhaling deeply, he lifted his head, trying to focus on the lyrics. More kissing, making love, asking her to be his bride… Reality came crashing down.

"Laura…I…this can't go anywhere…" he stammered in her ear, dropping his arms. He shouldn't be with her, shouldn't be touching her. Nothing could come of this. He had to make sure she knew that.

Grimacing, she looked at him. "I know. We're dancing, Hayden. We're friends. Let's enjoy the last few seconds, shall we?" She twirled away before she moved closer again. She was smiling, but she kept him at arm's length. As soon as the song was finished, she smiled vaguely at a spot somewhere above his head. "Thanks. You're a good dancer."

"There you are," Cooper said as he approached Laura and took her hand. "I haven't had a dance yet."

The music changed, and Cooper spun her away. Fed up with himself, his brother, and the whole ridiculous situation, Hayden made his way back to his mother. A hole the size of Texas opened up inside of him.

How the hell was he supposed to stop thinking about Laura? Wanting her? Because that, at least, he could admit to himself—he wanted her with every breath he took.

"Where's Luke?" he asked his mother. "We have to go."

"Sit down, Hayden," his mother said.

"I have to…"

"Sit. Down."

He sat down. The music was loud, so she moved closer.

"Hayden, my dear son, I love you dearly, as you well know, but at the moment, I want to hit you with something. As the oldest, you've always been the strong one, the one who kept everything together, even after our Walker died in that accident, even after Madeline passed away. You blame yourself for not protecting them, for not stopping what happened to them, but Hayden, sweetheart, you're not to blame. Nobody is. Bad things happen, people get ill. It's not anybody's fault. You can't go on hiding from life because you're scared of getting hurt again. That's not living."

She got up and held out her hand to Hayden. "Dance with your mother before you leave. Come on," she cajoled when he shook his head.

Cooper, the gentleman that he was, walked Laura to the front door of her house. She was still a little bit out of breath from all the dancing. They hadn't missed one and only stopped when the band packed up.

"Thank you for a lovely evening. I've really enjoyed it."

"Thank you for going with me." Smiling sheepishly, he rubbed the back of his neck. "Look, I know you and Hayden...what I mean is, I'm not sure what's going between you two, but I know my brother and he..." Cooper shook his head. "He can't stop looking at you. I was hoping if I invited you to the dance, he'd come to his senses and admit he feels something for you, but stubborn doesn't begin to describe him."

Laura couldn't help laughing. "So is this your way of telling me you only want to be friends?"

Cooper grinned. "Yes, please?"

"I'd love to be your friend. As for Hayden…" She shrugged. "I'm really happy on my own. I don't think I have what it takes to be in a relationship—the words of a previous boyfriend, by the way."

"Who is obviously an idiot. You and Hayden…"

But she didn't want to talk about him anymore or think about him either. "I was wondering about the dog you mentioned. I've more or less settled in, if it's still available? I was thinking of having a doggie door installed in the kitchen door, but I'm not sure how big it should be?"

"I can pick you up after school any day that suits you. You and Molly should meet first and see if the two of you hit it off."

Chewing her lip, she looked away. "I'm not sure about going to your ranch…"

"I have my own house. You don't have to see Hayden if you don't want to."

"Okay, but you don't have to pick me up. I can drive out to the ranch, so you don't have to…"

But Cooper was already shaking his head. "My mama will skin me alive. It gets dark way too soon and you don't know the roads. What about Friday? I'll put some steaks on

A FAMILY WITH THE COWBOY

the fire afterwards?"

She nodded. "Okay, thanks. I'd love to meet Molly."

With a smile and a wave, Cooper jogged down the stairs to his truck.

Cooper waited until she'd unlocked her front door before he drove away. Irritated and upset and sad and not sure why, she tucked her hair behind her ear. Cooper was attractive, kind, and caring. Why couldn't he wake up the butterflies in her tummy or send her blood roaring through her ears?

Sighing, she closed the door behind her. She had to forget about Hayden Weston, about men. Yes, judging from what she'd seen tonight, there were many other good-looking men in town she could probably date, although the idea of a night at home with a nice book or spending time with women friends was much more appealing to her. And when she had a dog, she'd have a companion.

But okay, maybe she should date. Occasionally, if anyone she liked asked her. It was a way to meet new people. But all these butterflies in the tummy, palpitations, and the way her whole body changed when Hayden was around was exhausting.

And who knew? Maybe there was another cowboy out there who'd send her heart into a frenzy. Maybe.

As she walked into her room, she caught herself humming. It was the tune she and Hayden had danced to. It was an oldie, one her dad used to love to listen to. She'd known there was a song about a guy kissing a girl in a way she'd never been kissed before. And then that was the song she and Hayden had danced to. Groaning out loud, she put her bag down. Hayden kissing her was so not something to be thinking about right now.

Her phone beeped. It was a text sent from an unknown number. Her heart stuttered to a halt before it valiantly tried to beat again. It was from Hayden. She knew that ever before she opened it.

You okay?

Her heart sighed, tears welling up behind her eyelids. Irritated, she wiped her eyes before she texted him back. She put her phone down and got undressed.

What was he trying to do, damn it? Right after she'd made up her mind to forget about him, he wanted to know if she was okay. He kept blowing hot and cold. The one minute he kissed her, the next, he wanted to make sure she knew nothing could ever happen between the two of them.

Upset, she walked to the bathroom. Steamy dreams about the big cowboy had already been keeping her awake over the past two weeks. How was she going to sleep tonight while she still vividly remembered every moment she'd danced with him?

You don't have to worry about me.

Hayden stared at Laura's text before he threw his phone down on the bed. What the hell had he expected? He was the one who'd wanted to make sure she knew nothing could happen between the two of them.

His gaze fell on the picture of Madeline he kept on his bedside table. Picking it up, he sat on the bed. They had all the time in the world, they'd thought. Maddie had wanted another baby, just before she became ill. But instead of growing old with the woman who'd stolen his heart, he was left to raise their son on his own.

"I miss you, Mads," he whispered, but the woman in the picture was gone. She couldn't respond.

He'd taken off his wedding ring last Christmas. He still wasn't sure what had finally made him do it. He had just known it was something he had to do.

His mom thought he feared getting hurt again, and maybe she was right. He'd learned the hard way happily-ever-after actually had an expiration date.

The real reason why he could never allow himself to fall for anyone else, he could never tell anyone. It was bad enough that he had to carry it with himself always: he couldn't even think of loving anyone ever again while his brother lay buried six feet deep, unable to ever experience the deep joy of loving someone and having that someone love you back.

Feeling guilty, he took Maddie's picture out of the frame, got up, and went to his closet, where he kept a photo album.

It didn't feel right to leave her picture next to his bed when he was dreaming of someone else.

Chapter Eleven

By the next Friday Laura was sleep-deprived, cranky, and ready to cry at the drop of a hat. On top of that, she was seriously worried about Luke. Something had obviously happened in the little boy's life since she'd seen him at the dance on Saturday, but she hadn't wanted to talk to him in front of the other kids, and of course she hadn't wanted to get in touch with his dad.

Arlene had texted on Sunday morning, inviting her again for lunch on Sunday, the day after the Winter Ball. Even though her whole being was craving to see Hayden again, she'd made arrangements with Ellie to go skating on Miracle Lake instead. If she was going to get the cowboy out of her mind, it would be best not to see him. A week tops, she argued. That was all she would need to forget about the kiss, the dancing, the warm, urgent lips trailing along her shoulder.

Except, she hadn't been able to forget about any of it, even for a second, over the past week. He'd haunted her dreams and every waking hour.

With a soft groan, she grabbed her bag. It was Friday.

A FAMILY WITH THE COWBOY

Cooper had promised to pick her up, and she had to persuade a dog to like her.

Luke was waiting outside her door. The little boy slipped a hand into hers. "I'm also going home with Cooper."

"That's nice." She smiled down at him, and for a few minutes, they walked in silence. "You want to tell me what's wrong?"

Luke was silent for another minute. "I miss my mom."

"Oh, sweetie, I know." Laura crouched down and hugged him. "I'm so sorry."

He pressed his face against her shoulder. "Dad put her picture away."

Laura hugged the little boy tighter, carefully considering what to say. "Have you asked him why he did that?"

Mumbling, Luke shook his head.

"Everyone handles grief differently, you know," she said, stroking his small back. "I'm sure he has a reason. Talk to him."

"He's been shouting a lot this week."

Swallowing her sigh, Laura got up. Cooper's truck was pulling up. "There's Cooper. Let's go." She'd thought Luke would run toward the truck, but his hand slipped into hers again. "Maybe your dad is worried about the ranch or something," she tried.

Amber eyes, so much like his dad's, looked up at her. "He likes you. But he doesn't want to. That's why he put Mom's picture away."

Before she could close her mouth, he was running toward Cooper.

Stunned, Laura followed slowly. Where in the world would Luke get an idea like that? There was no way Hayden would ever think something like that, let alone tell his son about it.

"Hi, Teach!" Cooper smiled as he walked around his truck to help her in. "Everything okay with Luke?" he asked below his breath.

She shook her head.

"He's not been himself all week," Cooper said under his breath as he helped her into the truck. "Any idea why?" He gave a lopsided smile. "Nobody is talking to Hayden this week. He's in a filthy mood."

"I…you'll have to ask him," she said softly.

Nodding, he closed her door before moving to his side of the truck. "Molly is excited to meet you," he said as he started the truck. "A little bit apprehensive, but excited."

"How do you know?"

"She's told him," Luke said as if it were the most natural thing in the world.

Smiling, Laura turned around to look at the little boy. "Don't tell me you also talk to animals?"

He rolled his eyes. "They don't talk-talk, Miss Anderson, but I know what they say."

Intrigued, she looked at Cooper. "So, how does it work?"

He shrugged. "It's different for everyone. We're all born

with the ability to understand animals, but most people lose that sense along the way."

Hesitantly, she turned around to look at Luke again. Could she ask him if he read people's minds, like his Aunt Willow?

The little boy smiled fleetingly at her before he looked out of the window. Blinking, Laura settled back into her seat. She was imagining things. Probably because of the lack of sleep.

"Where's Cooper?" Hayden asked as he sat down for dinner on Friday evening. He sounded irritated, he knew, but damn it, surely it couldn't be that difficult to be on time for meals?

"He's not coming," Willow said. "As you would know if you read your texts or listen to the conversation around the table. He fetched Laura and Luke earlier today from school. Laura and Molly are meeting to decide whether they like one another."

That freaking hole in Haden's chest grew bigger. Laura was with Coop again. "Who's Molly?" was all he asked, though.

"The rescue dog," Becket said. "Coop's been talking about it all week. How did you miss it?" Becket leaned over to Luke. "You're very quiet this week. Everything okay?"

Luke played with his food. "I miss Mom. Dad put her picture away."

Stunned, Hayden stared at his son. The thought that Luke might be upset because he'd removed Madeline's picture hadn't even entered his mind. He should've been more sensitive.

"You want him to put your mom's picture back?" Willow asked.

Sighing, Luke shook his head. "No, she's gone."

"I'll put it back," Hayden said.

Luke looked him straight in the eye. "I know why you put it away. It's okay. I'm going to play with Jessie now." He scooted off his chair and ran out of the kitchen, Jessie yapping at his heels.

Willow groaned out loud. "You know what that is?" she asked, pointing in the direction where Luke had disappeared.

"What do you mean?" Hayden asked.

"He has it as well."

"Has what?" Becket asked.

"Whatever I've inherited from our grandma. The ability to feel, to know what other people are feeling, what's going on in your minds."

"Don't be ridiculous," Hayden snapped.

But Willow wasn't listening anymore. As Hayden watched, her face turned stricken. He'd seen that particular expression often enough to know something was very wrong somewhere.

"Willow? What?" he asked as both he and Becket got up quickly.

"Someone is trying to start a fire…" Willow muttered.

"Where, Willow?" Hayden asked.

As if coming out of a trance, she stared at him. "The old barn. Someone is there…"

"Phone Coop!" Hayden shouted as he and Becket sprinted for the back door.

FRIDAY NIGHT AROUND eight, Laura was sitting, with Molly sleeping on her lap. They had just finished eating. She'd fallen in love with the little Jack Russell mix at first sight. Molly had been more hesitant. It took some cajoling to allow Laura to hold her. Initially, Molly had just shivered and wouldn't relax. Following Cooper's cue, Laura kept talking softly to the dog, kept stroking her until she'd eventually relaxed.

Frowning, Cooper suddenly got up slowly. Muttering, he picked up his phone.

"Cooper, is something wrong? I can try and get an Uber to come and fetch me."

"No, it's just…" he began, but his phone rang. Without looking who was calling him, he answered before the second ring. "Sis, what happened?"

By the time he put the phone in his pocket, he was clearly very worried. "I have to go. So sorry. Willow is coming to pick you up. We'll get you back home as soon as we can." And he was gone. Seconds later, his truck roared away.

Laura was still staring at the door, flabbergasted, when she heard the sound of another car stopping outside. Putting Molly down, she grabbed her coat and bag. "Sorry, sweetheart. I think you'd better stay here. I must still pay Cooper, but I'm coming back for you, okay?"

Molly licked her hand before she curled up on the couch. Laura hastened outside and closed the door behind her.

Willow was hanging halfway out of her truck and waved when she saw Laura. "Come on!"

"What's going on?" Laura asked as she rushed closer and got into the truck. Luke was sitting in the back seat, his face ashen in the light of the car. "You okay, sweetie?" she asked as Willow pulled away.

"Someone tried to start a fire at the old barn. I'm dropping you and Luke off at the big house before I also head that way. I've phoned the firehouse and the sheriff. Although Hayden and Becket have probably stopped the person in time, you never know. You'll look after Luke?"

"Of course," Laura said. "How did you know?"

Willow didn't answer her directly. "We were having dinner with Hayden when it happened."

"She just knows stuff," Luke said from the back.

"You also know stuff, don't you?" Willow asked.

"Not like you do," Luke said.

Willow didn't answer him, just stepping on the gas. Within minutes, she stopped in front of another house. "Keep your phone close, Laura. I'll let you know what's going on."

IT WAS AFTER midnight when Hayden returned to the homestead.

He was upset, frustrated, and tired. Leaving his boots on the porch, he entered the house. Laura should still be here somewhere. Willow had left her with Luke, his sister had said. Just the thought that she was here, somewhere in his house, was doing all sorts of strange things to his insides.

What a night. He'd never been so grateful for his sister's intuition, or whatever she wanted to call it. They'd been in time to stop Dan Smith before he could do too much damage. He had the match in his hand when they found him.

He'd tried to flee, but he ended up in a ditch just as Dawson O'Dell, the sheriff, arrived. At first, Smith had been tight-lipped until he'd heard what kind of jail time he might face for attempted arson.

He claimed Tim Higgins had paid him a lot of money to "burn the Weston Ranch to the ground." With Dan in the car with the sheriff and Hayden and his two brothers in his truck, they'd driven to Higgins Valley.

Of course, Tim had denied the whole thing. With only his word against Dan's, there wasn't really anything they could do, although Hayden had an appointment to see the sheriff tomorrow. They had to find a solution for Tim's problems before there was real damage. If that meant he had to press charges, then that was what he would do.

Hayden felt sick to his core. There was no doubt in his mind that Tim was behind the whole thing. Where Tim's fury and anger toward them stemmed from, he had no idea. They had tried to help him. He was the one who hadn't wanted their help.

Stretching his tired muscles, he took the stairs two at a time to the bedrooms on the second floor to check on Luke. As he opened the door to his son's room, he promptly lost his breath. Both Laura and Luke were fast asleep. Laura was lying next to his son, cradling him against her body, one of Luke's books lying open next to them. Luke's smaller hands were resting on top of Laura's.

He tried to inhale, but his chest seemed way too small. Damn. He'd tried all week to not think of her, but no matter how many hours he'd worked, how busy he'd been, she'd been on his mind the whole time. And at night she'd been center stage in his dreams as well.

Turning away quickly, he stumbled toward his own room, needing a shower and then his bed.

Chapter Twelve

LAURA OPENED HER eyes slowly. For a moment, she didn't know where she was. As unfamiliar sounds from outside penetrated the sleepy haze she'd been in, she sat up. She was in Hayden's house on the ranch.

Luke had been scared last night and worried, so after he'd had a shower, she'd put him to bed and sat next to him on the bed to read him a story. It was only during the third story that he'd finally fallen asleep.

She had to have fallen asleep, as well, right after he did. The little sleep of the week before had finally caught up with her.

Rubbing her face, she called out to Luke. He was nowhere to be seen, though. She checked her watch. Oh my gosh, it was already past nine.

Grabbing her phone, she jumped up and ordered an Uber before she headed to the nearest bathroom. It would be nice to at least brush through her hair and wash her face. Fortunately, she always carried a moisturizer and the basic makeup in her bag. A shower would've been nice, but standing naked anywhere in Hayden's house was so not a good idea. Oh, my goodness, so not something she should be thinking about now.

A few minutes later, feeling fresher, she jogged down the stairs and followed the sound of Luke's voice. He was on the kitchen floor playing with two dogs, one who looked a lot like Molly. And sitting at the kitchen table, drinking coffee, looking drop-dead gorgeous in a denim shirt and faded jeans, was Hayden. Amber eyes found hers.

He got up. "Come and sit. There's coffee and fresh scones. Isabella doesn't usually come in on a Saturday, so you're in for a treat."

The dog that looked a lot like Molly saw her and, tail wiggling, came hesitantly closer. Smiling, Laura crouched down. "Thanks. I've phoned Maria. She's picking me up soon."

Hayden chuckled, the mere sound sending delicious shivers down her spine. "You don't have to rush off. I'll take you."

Ignoring him, she looked down at the dog trying to climb on her lap. "Look who's here. Hi, Molly." Picking up the dog, she cuddled her close.

"And this is Jessie. She's my dog," Luke said. Sniffing, Jessie cautiously approached Laura.

"Coop brought the dog this morning," Hayden said. "According to him, you and Molly have decided to give living together a go. He's also left two bags of stuff for her, including a doggie door. I'll install it when I drop you off.

Tell Maria I'll take you. I have to go into town, anyway, to see Dawson O'Dell, the sheriff."

"Don't worry about it. It's totally fine. I…" She put Molly down before she stood, only to find Hayden standing right in front of her with a mug of coffee in his hand.

He combed her hair from her face. "I'll take you. You stayed with Luke last night. It's the least I can do."

Her legs had turned to mush. "O-okay." With hands not quite steady, she took out her phone and texted Maria.

After she'd put her phone in the pocket of her jeans, he handed her the mug. Her fingers grazed his as she took it. Inhaling sharply, she met his eyes. Whether it was her imagination or real, Laura didn't know, but the whole kitchen was alive with all sorts of strange vibrations.

"Good morning, Miss Anderson," a woman said behind Laura.

Grateful for the interruption, Laura quickly turned around. She'd met the friendly Isabella a few times when the older woman had picked Luke up from school. "Laura, please. Good morning."

"Sit down, both of you," Isabella ordered. "I'm making breakfast."

"Oh, please, it's really not…"

Isabella grabbed her hands. "You stayed with Luke last night. Of course I'm making you breakfast."

Hayden pulled out a chair, his eyes crinkling at the corners from his smile. "From experience, I can tell you this isn't a fight you're going to win."

"I don't want to be a bother, really…"

"Please sit down?" Hayden asked. "You'll always bother me," he said under his breath as she sat.

She glanced at him, but he was already walking toward his chair. Had he really said that or was she hearing things now?

TWO HOURS LATER, Hayden turned into the driveway in front of Laura's house. Before the car had properly stopped, she'd already opened the door.

"Laura, damn it," he growled as he also got out. "You wanna get killed?"

She had the dog in one arm and was struggling to take out both bags Cooper had left for the dog from the back of the truck. "I've taken up so much of your time. Thanks for the lift. Don't worry about the doggie door. I'll…"

Gnashing his teeth, he walked around his truck and took the bags from her. "I said I'll do it."

Muttering under her breath, she stomped past him toward the front porch. "It's clear you can't get rid of me quickly enough. You haven't said a word all the way from the ranch. You really don't have to bother…" After unlocking the door, she turned around and held out her hand to take the bags from him.

"I've told you, you're always going to bother me," he said, moving past her so that he could get into the house. "I haven't had talking on my mind. Which door is going to get the doggie door?" Dropping the bags on the floor and his jacket on a chair, he turned to look at her.

"Hayden, seriously," she began hotly, those blue eyes shooting lightning. She put down the dog and took off her coat. "I said—"

Sighing in surrender, he slowly pulled her closer, giving her ample time to push him away if she wanted to. This was why he was here. To kiss her, to touch her, to hold her in his arms.

"Hayden, what—?"

"I don't wanna talk. Kissing you is what I've been dreaming about and thinking about all damn week. But if you don't want this…"

"Oh, for goodness' sake, just kiss me already," she muttered as she grabbed his shirt in both her hands.

"Yes, ma'am." He smiled. Cupping her face in his hands, he kissed her. With his blood roaring in his ears, he swallowed her gasp and deepened the kiss. Her lips were soft and warm, her body fitting perfectly against his. Only when she melted against him did he lift his head.

"Wanting to do this has been driving me crazy," he said. "You and I need to talk, but I have an appointment with the sheriff about last night. Dinner, tonight? I'll pick you up at seven. So, which door gets the doggie door?"

"Doggie door?" Laura stared at him, looking so gorgeous, he had to kiss her again.

With a groan, he gathered her close. "You're killing me, you know that?" he murmured against her lips before he kissed her again.

His blood heated instantly, and, steeped in her scent, her softness, his hands slid down her back and he pulled her close against him, making sure she knew exactly what she did to him.

The loud yapping of a dog finally penetrated his mind. Molly had had enough of being ignored and was jumping up against Laura's legs.

Frowning, Laura bent down to pick up the dog and glared at him. It didn't quite work, with her lips still swollen with his kisses and desire still lurking in her eyes. "Now you want to kiss? Saturday night, you made sure I knew nothing can happen between us. You haven't spoken a word to me while driving from the ranch, but now you want to install a doggie door, and you keep kissing me!"

"Don't you want me to kiss you?"

"Of course, I want to kiss… argh! You make me so mad, I say things I shouldn't say. I was perfectly happy on my own and then you stormed into my classroom, all broody and sexy and angry, and I haven't stopped thinking about you since!"

"Sexy, uh?" he drawled.

"That is so not the point!" she cried out. "You blow hot

and cold, and I never know what is going to happen next. I've been trying to get you out of my mind…"

Sighing, he rubbed his face. "I never expected…you. I've also tried ignoring you, but it's not working. All I can think about is you. Kissing you, being with you. I've been married. You know that. I have a son. On top of that, there's Walker. He is dead because…and he would never be able…" With a sigh, he shook his head. "And I couldn't talk to you on the way here, because I don't wanna talk. I wanna kiss you. But there is no future in whatever this is between us. I was hoping, though, we can figure this out. I can't think straight with wanting to be with you." He glanced at his watch. "But right now, I have to install the damn doggie door so that I can leave. Before I forget about all my responsibilities and take you to your room, to that big bed, the one I helped carry in there, and make love to you until neither of us can see straight."

For another second, she stared at him. "Figure it out? You mean, have a fling?"

"I… that's not really what I mean, but okay, maybe that's not a bad idea. Maybe we can get this thing between us out of our systems and—"

"There is nothing to figure out," she interrupted him, her eyes bright. "Either you want to be with me, or you don't. I don't do flings. I'm not something you 'get out of your system,' as you've put it so eloquently. You having a son isn't the complication, and you know it. You're obviously carrying a lot of baggage around and I've had enough of men with issues to last me a lifetime. I can't fix you. I can't help you with your baggage. We're both healthy adults. We have hormones. It will settle at some point. We will just keep on ignoring whatever this is until it goes away. So no, thank you, I'm not going to dinner with you, I'm not having a fling with you, and I'm not falling for you while you're trying to figure out what you're feeling." She pointed toward the back door. "That door, I think. The back is enclosed, so Molly should be fine during the day when I'm at school. Please close the front door on your way out."

With Molly still in her arms, she turned away and walked out of the kitchen.

Flabbergasted, Hayden stared after her. Well, hell. This was not how he'd thought the morning would end.

Clenching his teeth, he grabbed the tools. He'd never understand women. Best to stay as far away from them as possible. He was trying to be honest, to be straight with her up front, but clearly, she wasn't interested.

LAURA MANAGED TO keep busy in her room until she heard Hayden's truck drive away. As the sound faded, she sat down on the bed and the first tear rolled down her cheek. No, damn it, she wasn't going to cry. She tried to wipe it away, but a sob from deep within her body escaped and then she was crying. Curling onto her side, she lay down on the bed and sobbed into the pillow.

Molly, who had been sleeping on Laura's bed, crawled over to her and began to lick her face.

Rubbing Molly behind the ears, Laura laughed on a sob. "Oh, sweetie, look at me, crying over a man. What nonsense." Wiping her tears away, she stood up with Molly in her arms. "Let's go and find something to eat."

Grabbing her phone from the bedside table, she moved toward the door. The phone slipped through her fingers, but before it could drop to the floor, she managed to get a good enough grip on it so that she could put it into her pocket.

Sniffing, she hugged Molly. "Look at me, all teary and miserable. That's going to change right now. You and I, Molly, we have each other. I don't want a man who wants to be with me only to get me out of his system. If…and that's a big if, mind you, I fall in love, it will be with someone who wants to be with me, always. 'Get me out of his system.' Who says that, anyway?"

The doggie door had been installed and Hayden had also cleaned up after himself. "Look, Molly, you have a door. Let's practice." As she bent down with Molly, her phone dropped to the floor. The front was lit up, and she switched if off before she left it on the table. "Come on, let's try the door."

MUTTERING AND STOMPING his feet to get off the snow, Hayden put a hand on the door to the sheriff's offices. What the hell had he been thinking, anyway? The problem was, when he was with Laura, he didn't think at all. Other parts of his body worked fine, just not his brain.

His phone rang. Irritated, he took it out of his pocket and dropped his hand from the door. It was a call from Laura.

"You okay?" he asked, but she didn't answer.

He was inhaling to ask her again if she was okay when he heard her voice. A second later he realized she didn't know that she'd dialed his number. It was a "butt call," as Becket called it. Turning away from the building, he listened to her voice as she talked to Molly.

Minutes later, he put the phone back in his pocket.

I don't want a man who wants to be with me only to get me out of his system. If...and that's a big if, mind you, I fall in love, it will be with someone who wants to be with me, always.

What if he wanted to be with her, but he couldn't? What if—

"Hayden?" a voice asked behind him. It was Dawson, holding the door. "Come on in. It's cold out there."

"Thanks," Hayden muttered as he entered the station. He had enough trouble as it was. He didn't need another complication.

Chapter Thirteen

"Has Luke left for school already?" Hayden asked as he sat down to have breakfast. Only Becket's dogs were lying near him, as always. Jessie was nowhere to be seen. They'd all been up since early this morning. It was Monday, two weeks since he'd installed the doggie door for Laura—two weeks of restless nights and endless days thinking about her.

It was the last week of March. The spring equinox had come and gone, but the weather was moody. Some days it was warm and gentle, followed by angry winds and dark skies—kinda like his own mood. They had just experienced another heavy snowfall with freezing temperatures. Outside, the ground was becoming sodden and heavy. The brief periods of above-freezing temperatures only aggravated the problem of weight of snow on the many roofs on the ranch. On a ranch the work never stopped.

"Don't you remember?" Isabella pulled out a chair and sat down with a mug of coffee. "It's school break this week."

"Of course." Feeling like an idiot, Hayden shook his head. He should know what was going on in his son's life, damn it.

Becket slapped him on the shoulder as he got up. "You're in a filthy mood, bro. I don't know what your problem is, but you've moved from grumpy to downright insufferable. Everyone, even Ricardo, is complaining about your temper. I'm tired of trying to explain your behavior."

"Mind your own damn business," Hayden growled.

"You are literally our business," Coop said mildly, as he also got up. "It's about time you admit what is bugging you so that we can get on with the business of ranching. I want to show you something in the barn, Becket."

Both his brothers left the kitchen.

Isabella also got up.

Hayden glared at her. "You also have a complaint?"

"I agree with your brothers," she said stiffly before she also left the kitchen.

"What about you?" he snarled at Willow.

"Oh, I know what your problem is. We all do."

"Yeah? And what is that?"

"You've got a thing for the lovely Laura, but you're too stubborn to admit it or…"

"Damn it, I've admitted it. I've told her. She's not interested."

Willow's eyes widened. "Really? What exactly have you told her?"

Fed up, Hayden crossed his arms. "I've tried to be honest. There is no future in whatever is between us, but I thought we could spend time together."

Groaning out loud, Willow rolled her eyes. "Good for her for blowing you off. You don't tell a woman like Laura, 'Hey babe, let's have a fling for a while.' Who does that? You should be ashamed of yourself."

Muttering under his breath, he rubbed his face. "I wasn't the one who called it a fling. She used the word. I don't see what's wrong with spending time together. Anyway, it's a moot point. She's not interested."

Willow shook her head. "Look, I am the last person to talk about relationships. You know I can never have one. But you feel something for her. I have an idea it's not the kind of feeling that will just go away and a fling isn't going to 'cure' you, if that's what you're thinking. You feel deeply, Hayden. You always have. It's not going to go away after a few kisses."

"I've discovered that."

"Ah, so you've kissed her?"

He glared at her. "Don't you know these things?"

"Not everything, but I do know what you're feeling right now isn't temporary."

He got up quickly. "Well, it'll have to be. I can't go through losing someone again." The words were out before he'd thought about it.

"And there you have it." Willow nodded as she stood up. "The reason why you're running scared. Understandably so. It's not the only reason, of course." She shrugged. "I'm just glad you've told Laura there's no future for you two. I was wondering why she's dating just about every single guy in town over the past two weeks. Now it makes sense." And with a wave of her hand, she walked out of the kitchen.

Stunned, Hayden stared after her. Laura was dating? Somehow, the thought hadn't entered his mind. But now… Indignant, he stormed out of the kitchen. A fling with him was out of the question, but she was dating other men?

Outside, he gulped in the cold air. The weather suited his mood. He missed Laura with a fierceness that staggered him.

From the direction of the barn came the sound of Luke's laughter and Jessie's barking. Since Laura had taken over from Mrs. Denton, Luke had lost the gloomy and sad air that had become part of him over the past two years. He was happy and laughing. The only problem was, he never stopped talking about Laura.

The past two Sundays during lunch with his mother, Luke had disappeared. When he'd returned, he'd been all smiles. He'd seen Miss Anderson and played with Molly, he'd told them, beaming from ear to ear.

Trudging through the sodden, muddy snow toward the barn, Hayden rubbed his chest where a huge hole had opened up, one that was growing bigger by the day.

Surely, there was an expiration date for whatever it was that kept Laura in his thoughts and dreams? He couldn't go on like this.

As he entered the barn, he saw Willow with Luke. They

were deep in conversation. As he neared them, Luke saw him. His smiled slipped and he moved closer to his aunt.

Sighing, Hayden held out a hand to his son. "I haven't seen you this morning."

"Are you gonna yell again?" Luke asked.

Willow's lips twitched.

"No, I..." Sighing, he crouched down. "Come here."

Warily, Luke glanced up at his aunt. Only after she'd nodded did Luke walk closer to him.

Hayden pulled him closer and combed his hair out of his face. "I've forgotten there's no school this week. What about you and I drive into town a little bit later this morning and go get ourselves a hot chocolate from Copper Mountain Chocolates?"

"Do you have time?" Luke asked.

"I'm making time. Especially if you help me with the chores before we go?"

For the first time, a smile lit up Luke's face. "Yes! Come on, Jessie, let's go!" He ran outside, Jessie on his heels.

As Hayden and Willow walked out of the barn, a truck parked near the entrance.

MONDAY MORNING, JUST after nine, Laura closed the front door behind her. The fire in the living room was warm and cozy, but she seemed unable to get warm. Maybe she should try to clear her head before she tried to warm up.

It was freezing outside, but she was wrapped up for the cold, with the scarf she'd finished knitting around her neck. Her house seemed strangely small since the school break. It was time to get outside. Even though the last two weeks had been extremely busy as she had tried to catch up with everything at school, she missed Hayden with every breath she took.

It also didn't help that she saw his son, who had his father's eyes, every day. Luke didn't miss much. On Friday he'd given her a fierce hug and said he hoped she wouldn't be sad anymore when he saw her again.

Why couldn't she stop thinking about Hayden? Yes, he was attractive, but she'd dated other attractive men, and as soon as they'd parted ways, they'd disappeared from her mind as well. But this time, he seemed to be stuck there and just about everything reminded her of him.

"Come on, Molly. I know it's cold, but let's take a quick walk around the block."

Molly barked as she skipped down the steps. For the first few days, Molly had been unsure of her surroundings, shivering and cowering at the slightest loud sound. The little dog was already much better, but Laura had learned to speak softly and be very gentle with her. Getting Molly to use the doggie door was difficult—and not only because the poor thing was scared to go through it initially. Even the freaking doggie door reminded her of Hayden.

A FAMILY WITH THE COWBOY

The sky was gray, with Copper Mountain hiding behind thick, dark clouds, but she simply couldn't stare at the walls for one more second. It wasn't as if she didn't have enough to do. There was a long list of things she didn't get to during school term.

The house wasn't quite hers yet, but the process had begun. Although the place was in mint condition, there were smaller changes she'd like to make. She'd like more cupboards in the kitchen. Arlene would probably know a cabinetmaker in town she could recommend.

But…somehow, she was struggling to focus, because... Groaning out loud, she walked down the steps. Because she kept thinking about Hayden Weston.

She hadn't seen him since he'd left her house two weeks ago. Over the last ten days, she'd said yes to every guy who'd asked her out on a date. There had to be at least one other man who could wake up the butterflies in her tummy, she'd convinced herself. It turned out, though, nobody else had any effect on her tummy or any other part of her body.

Some were nice, some were dull, some were funny, others so boring she wanted to cry in her food. After two weeks she had to admit there was only one guy who heated her blood, but all he wanted was a fling.

Deep in thought, she and Molly reached the sidewalk in front of her house. Molly was happily sniffing and in no big hurry.

A fling. She'd never thought of herself as a let's-have-a-fling kind of gal, but over the last few days she'd been wondering if maybe there was something to be said for the idea.

Maybe Hayden was right. Get naked and sleep together... well, sleeping was obviously not going to do the trick. Have sex.

Vivid images of Hayden's naked upper body—the one she hadn't even seen yet and probably never would—popped into her mind.

Oh, my goodness, this wasn't helping. Inhaling shakily, she looked up and down the street. Which way would they go?

"It's Tim Higgins," Willow said as they walked toward the truck. "Do you want me to call Dawson?"

Just then, Hayden's two brothers appeared from behind the barn. Thank goodness Luke was gone for the moment. "It's fine. Coop and Becket are here as well."

Tim got out of his truck, clearly looking uncomfortable.

"Higgins," Hayden said curtly.

After a glance in Cooper and Becket's direction, Tim looked at Hayden. "I wanna talk to you."

"So talk."

"In private."

His siblings stepped closer. "This is as private as it's going to get," Hayden said.

"No complaint has been filed against me, Dawson O'Dell tells me."

"Not yet."

Higgins sniggered. "No evidence, I take it."

"You'd be wrong."

"What? If you ask me, all you have is your crazy sister's…"

Both Cooper and Becket stepped closer to Higgins.

Staggering backward, he pointed his finger toward them. "You're all crazy. The lot of you. I don't know how, but you're using my land for grazing for your cattle. I just know it. That's why we're having problems. This ridiculous grazing system you're promoting is BS and I'll prove it. You've taken what's mine, so don't think I'm done with you."

This time Hayden moved forward. Tim quickly got into his truck. As he drove away, Luke and Jessie came running around the corner.

For an excruciating moment, everything happened in slow motion. Higgins's truck swerved to the left, toward the boy and his dog. Because of the angle they were standing, Hayden couldn't see whether Tim's car had hit Luke, but he heard his little boy's cries.

He was running even before Tim's truck stopped. "Luke!" he roared, with the sound of his siblings' shouts behind him.

They all reached Luke simultaneously. His son was on

his knees next to Jessie, crying. The dog was lying very still.

"I'm sorry..." Tim was saying behind them. "I didn't mean it, I was just so...so angry."

"Get the hell off our ranch," Becket said.

"But I'm so sorry..."

Hayden ignored Tim. His only concern was his son.

"I didn't mean..." Tim's voice again. "Is the boy okay?"

"Just go, please?" Willow's voice.

"Sorry..." Tim muttered as he walked back to his truck.

"I'm phoning Dawson." Becket had his phone out.

Hayden shook his head. "Leave it. I'll talk to Tim when I know Luke is fine."

"That man hurt Jessie!" Luke cried and moved to pick up Jessie.

"Don't touch him," Cooper stopped Luke as he and Willow crouched down next to Jessie. Cooper put his hands on the dog.

Hayden was on his knees in front of Luke. "Are you okay?" Fear still clutching his throat, he ran his hands down his son's arms. "Have you been hurt?" Luke was deathly pale and he was shivering.

"Not me...Jessie," Luke sobbed as he turned back toward his dog.

Tim's truck pulled away.

Becket put his phone away. "Damn it, Hayden, I don't know why you don't want to phone Dawson. This time 'round, you have to press charges. Where does he get the idea our cattle graze on their land?"

His heart still racing, Hayden got up. "They're struggling."

"I know you're sorry for his wife, but he's clearly unstable," Becket said.

Ignoring his brother, Hayden took Luke's hand. He'd talk to Tim when he knew his son was okay. "Come on buddy, I'm taking you to the hospital…"

"No!" Luke cried, his eyed wide with fear.

Willow quickly stepped closer. "What if Dad takes you to Doctor Vivian's house where she sees patients?"

Hayden swallowed. Of course. The last time Luke had been to Marietta Regional Hospital was the day before Madeline had passed away. "Good idea. Will you please phone her?" he asked Willow.

Willow nodded, her phone already in her hand. "Of course. Drive safely."

"What about Jessie?" Luke cried, turning back to where Cooper was still sitting next to the dog.

"The vet is on his way," Cooper said, putting his phone away. "I think Jessie is going to be fine. We'll do everything we can, I promise."

"Come on, Luke. Let's get you out of those wet clothes before we leave."

Chapter Fourteen

BY THE TIME Laura and Molly had walked around the block, she was shivering from the cold. Picking up Molly, she walked faster. "Let's get home. It's the perfect day for getting back into bed and reading. There is still soup…"

As they neared Vivian and Aiden's house, she noticed the truck driving down the street. Her heart missed a beat. If she wasn't mistaken, it was Hayden's truck. Arlene's front door opened and her neighbor came rushing out, pulling on her coat as she ran down the stairs.

Laura's heart tripped. Something was wrong. As the truck turned and parked in the driveway in front of Vivian's and Aiden's house, she ran closer, Molly still in her arms. Something was wrong. Luke or Hayden…

She and Arlene reached the truck simultaneously. Laura put Molly down. Arlene opened the door on the passenger side and hugged Luke. "Luke, sweetie…" she cried.

Hayden came around his truck, looking grave and shaken.

"What happened?" His mouth opened and closed a few times. He was clearly deeply upset. Without thinking, Laura stepped closer and hugged him. "What happened?" she asked against his chest.

With a groan, he pulled her closer and pressed his face into her shoulder. Stroking his back with her one hand, she tried to convey how much she'd missed him, how sorry she was for whatever has happened.

"Hayden…" Arlene's voice finally penetrated the bubble Laura was sharing with Hayden.

He stepped closer to his mom, giving her a hug before he took Luke's hand. "Doctor Vivian is going to make sure Luke here is okay. We had a scare just now, didn't we, buddy?"

"Jessie was hurt." Luke sniffed. "I tried to grab her away from the wheel of that man's truck, but…" Tears streamed down his face.

Laura crouched down and hugged him. "I'm so sorry you had to see that. Let's make sure you're all right and then we'll find out about Jessie, okay?"

"Will you come with me?"

"We're going to crowd poor Doctor Vivian's office. But I'll phone later to find out how you are, okay?"

"'Kay."

The front door opened and Vivian stepped out, smiling. "Good morning. Come on in. Hi, Luke." She held out her hand to the little boy.

"She's so good with kids," Arlene said while Vivian spoke to Luke. "You go with them, Hayden. I'll tell Laura what happened before I join you."

Hayden's gaze met hers briefly before he turned and walked into the house with Vivian and his son.

"Willow called a few minutes ago," Arlene said, dabbing at her eyes. "Tim Higgins arrived on the ranch this morning…" She quickly explained what had happened. "Will you excuse me, please? I want to hear what Vivian says."

"Of course. We'll talk later."

With a wave, Arlene disappeared into the house and closed the front door. Molly was now also shivering. "Let's go home, sweetie. I hope Luke is okay. He's so pale."

With her mind racing in circles, she walked home. The house was nice and warm inside. Molly immediately stretched herself in front of the fire.

Laura couldn't settle down. The long list of things she should be doing was out of her mind. All she could think about was Luke. He was so pale. And then there was the memory of Hayden's arms around her, his warm breath on her neck. The whole incident probably only lasted a few seconds, but she remembered everything.

With a groan, she walked toward the kitchen. Warm tea sounded nice. She couldn't believe what Tim Higgins had done. If she remembered correctly, he was the same man who'd hit Hayden at the Winter Ball. The guy was obviously unstable. Why would he do something like that?

While the kettle heated, she looked out of the window. Hayden's truck was still parked in Vivian's driveway and there was no sign of Arlene.

IT WAS ONLY when they were leaving Vivian's office that Hayden's heart settled down. He'd convinced himself Luke had somehow been injured and had waited for Vivian to give the verdict. Why was his son so pale?

He'd been really scared, Vivian explained, but she'd checked all his vitals and was satisfied that his heart rate and his blood pressure were fine, and he wasn't in shock. Apart from a scrape on his one knee, he was unharmed. The color had returned to his face and over the last few minutes, he'd stopped asking about Jessie.

Just then, his phone rang. It was Cooper.

"That's Uncle Coop," Luke said, without looking at Hayden's phone. "Jessie will be okay."

"Hi, Coop," Hayden answered.

"Jessie is fine," Cooper said. "But I have an idea Luke knows that."

Resignedly, Hayden shook his head. "I'm not even going to ask how you know or he knows, but he's just told me."

"And Luke's okay?"

Hayden chuckled. "He's okay. Next time, I'll skip going to the doctor and just ask you or Willow."

"What about you?"

"What about me?"

"Still grumpy?"

Hayden glanced in the direction of Laura's house. Those few seconds he'd held her in his arms would forever stay in his heart, but nothing had changed. Everything inside him was urging him to go to her, talk to her, kiss her, but he couldn't give her what she wanted.

"Nothing has changed. We're on our way."

"You sure you don't need to make another stop?" Cooper asked.

"Good-bye, Coop." Shaking his head, he took Luke's hand. "Let's go home."

"Can I go and tell Miss Anderson I'm okay?"

"I don't think…" Hayden began.

"Wonderful idea," his mom interrupted. "She was so worried."

He could easily ignore his mother, but ignoring his son's pleading eyes was more difficult. "Okay, but we can't stay, okay? Get in the truck, let's go."

"'Kay." Luke sighed.

Minutes later, he parked in front of Laura's house. His mother and Luke got out.

Laura's front door opened before his mom could knock. She'd probably heard the truck's engine.

"Luke!" she cried and crouched down. "I'm so happy to see you. Come on in."

"Dad says we can't stay," Luke said.

Laura's gaze met his for a brief second, but it was long

enough for him to see the hurt.

Laura looked at Luke again. "You okay?"

"I'm okay."

Laura held out her arms. "May I please hug you? I've been so worried."

Luke fell into her arms and hugged her tightly. Hayden had to swallow against the lump in his throat. It was the way Luke used to hug his mom.

"…a book for you," Laura said, before she disappeared into the house.

His mother looked at him, shaking her head. "I can't decide whether you're stubborn or dumb or both."

Before he could react, Laura was back with a few books for Luke. Inhaling deeply, Luke took them from her. "Thank you, Miss Anderson."

"You can bring them back after the break." She smiled.

"Laura, I'd like to come in if I may?" his mother asked. "I want to ask you about that knitting pattern I got from you. We have our knitting group again tomorrow night and I've been struggling," she explained to Hayden.

Laura didn't meet Hayden's eyes. "Of course. Come on in, I've just made tea."

Ignoring Luke's pleading eyes, he took his son's hand. "I have to get back," he said, without looking at Laura or his mom again.

Even before he'd started the truck, the front door was closed. Irritated, he reversed the truck.

"You like Miss Anderson," Luke said.

"She's nice."

"She likes you too."

"How do you know?"

Luke gave him a look, one he'd seen before in his sister's and brother's eyes. He just knew.

Frowning, Hayden stepped on the gas. He hadn't picked up before today that Luke seemed to have Willow's and Cooper's ability to see beyond the ordinary. For the past two years, he'd just concentrated on putting one foot before the other and dealing with his grief.

He wasn't as freaked out by Willow's ability as he used to be when they were kids. Although, to be honest, he was still uncomfortable talking about it. He'd long ago realized to trust his sister's gut, though, since she was always right. And Cooper had this thing with animals. Horses, cattle, dogs, cats, even wild animals all had a special bond with his youngest brother. Cooper also knew things. He just wasn't as vocal about it as their sister.

So what did he do? Talk to Luke about it? Talk to Willow? Maybe Laura…?

He quickly dismissed the thought as soon as it popped into his mind. Although she occupied his thoughts every waking moment of his day and even while he was sleeping, he should stay away from her.

"…it will be with someone who wants to be with me, always." Laura's words echoed in his mind. And that was the

problem. He couldn't give her want she wanted.

It had only been two weeks. He should give it time.

"So, do you have big plans for your week off, or are you going to spend it reading?" Arlene asked as she and Laura settled in front of the fire with their tea.

Laura laughed. "That does sound wonderful, but I do have things I want to do around the house. That wall, for instance," she said, pointing toward the one wall opposite them, "needs a different color, I think. And then maybe add one or two kitchen cabinets. I was wondering if you can recommend someone?"

"Ooh," Arlene said, taking out her phone. "I do know of someone you can ask. Tanner Olsen. Let me phone him immediately…"

"No, really, that's…" Laura tried, but Arlene was already talking on the phone.

Within minutes, she put her phone down with a smile. "He's on his way. Get a quote, see if you like him, but I know his mother. They're good people. So, Laura," she said, putting her cup down. "You and Hayden? Is there something between the two of you?"

"Wow." Laura smiled, shaking her head. "You really get to the point, don't you?"

"Life is so very short, my dear. If you have something to

say, say it. I'd like to think we've become friends. You do like him, don't you?"

"Yes, I like him. I like your whole family. I'm looking forward to tomorrow night. I haven't seen Ellie since last month. Have you finished reading *Pride and Prejudice* for the discussion?"

Arlene sighed. "Okay. You don't want to talk about it. I get it. It just breaks my heart when I see two people who should be together, but who are so scared to take a chance, they walk away."

"Hayden is still mourning his wife and brother. Besides, he's made it clear he's not looking for anything permanent."

"Really?"

"His words. Now about *Pride and Prejudice*..."

Fortunately, this time, Arlene let her change the topic of conversation. She'd hoped—she'd really, really hoped—the hug Hayden had given her meant something, but he had been worried about Luke, and she'd offered a shoulder. That was it.

This was a clear sign that she should stop dreaming about the cowboy with the sad eyes. He'd have to come to grips with his demons all by himself. She couldn't do it for him.

Minutes later, there was a knock on the front door.

"That's probably Tanner," Arlene said, as she put down her cup. "I'll leave you two together." Her eye twinkled. "Have I mentioned that he's very attractive?"

Laughing, Laura moved toward the front door. "I thought Janice was the matchmaker in town."

"Just saying," Arlene chuckled, as Laura opened the door.

The guy standing on her porch was indeed attractive. Tall, well-built, blonde hair, brown eyes, wide shoulders, and a lopsided grin—he was the quintessential handsome guy. But there were no crackling vibes and not even one butterfly in her tummy stirred.

Molly ran closer, barking furiously.

"Molly!" Laura cried and quickly picked up the dog. "Sorry about that."

Grinning, he cautiously put out a hand to Molly, but she growled and showed her teeth.

Arlene introduced them. "Laura, Tanner. Tanner, Laura. And this fierce protector is Molly. Thanks for the tea, my dear. Oh, and Tanner—Laura is new to town. I don't think she's been to Rocco's Italian Restaurant yet."

"Arlene!" Laura cried out, but Arlene was already briskly walking away.

Tanner grinned. "Great idea."

Groaning, Laura opened the door wider. "Seriously, you don't have to. And I actually have been there recently. It seems everyone in town is trying to be a matchmaker. Come on in."

"I've seen you around town and was still trying to figure out a way to meet you when Arlene phoned. Let's look at what you need done and then we can talk about going out to dinner soon?"

By the time Tanner was leaving, Laura was excited about the project. Tanner obviously knew what he was talking about and had even offered to paint the wall for her, free of charge. She would pay him, nonetheless, but she appreciated the nice gesture to a stranger. His suggestion of freestanding cabinets she could move how and when she wanted to made sense.

Molly hadn't warmed to the stranger, though. Laura eventually had to put her in the bedroom. Since then, the little dog's heart-wrenching barks, mixed with indignant yelps, hadn't stopped for a moment.

"So, how about Friday night?" He grinned as he walked out on to the porch. "I would really like to take you to Rocco's. If you've been there, you'll know the pizzas are great."

"Look, just because Arlene…"

"I'd really like to take you. It doesn't have anything to do with Arlene."

"Okay, thanks. I love their pizza."

"A girl after my own heart." He smiled. "I'll pick you up at around seven?"

"Thank you."

With a smile, he turned around and jogged down to his truck.

Laura closed the front door. Tanner was a nice guy. It would be okay. Hayden was obviously so over whatever he'd felt for her, and it was time for her to move on too.

Happily-ever-after didn't exist in real life—something she'd discovered when her mom died.

Molly was still barking. Laura quickened her steps and opened the bedroom door. Molly stopped mid-bark and jumped off the bed. Laura crouched down to pick her up, but she sidestepped her, and with another bark, stormed out of the room.

Only when she was satisfied the stranger had left did she return to Laura.

"That was very bad behavior," Laura scolded.

Molly lay down on the floor and put her paws over her face. Laughing, Laura scooped her up. Why would Molly bark at Tanner? She should remember to leave her in the room again Friday night.

TUESDAY NIGHT, THEY didn't get any knitting or crocheting done at Ellie's. Everyone wanted to talk about Tim Higgins and what had happened on Hayden's ranch.

"I still don't know why Hayden didn't call the sheriff!" Annie said, clearly very upset after hearing the story from Willow.

Willow shook her head. "Hayden has always been a peacemaker. He had already decided not to press charges when Tim's wife called him yesterday morning, crying and pleading her husband's case. The ranching community of Marietta has always supported each other, so Tim's behavior is so unexpected."

"So what now?" Vivian asked. "He gets off scot-free?"

Willow grimaced. "Well, Tim and his wife are coming to the ranch on Friday. Hayden wants to talk to them and offer our help again. It was what Dad would've wanted, he says."

Arlene patted her daughter's hand. "So true. Your father always tried to settle conflict before it spiraled out of control."

"And Becket and Cooper?" asked Annie. "Do they agree?"

Willow shrugged. "Becket isn't very happy about the whole thing, but Hayden has convinced him to try. I'm also for it. Ranching is hard work. There's no time for petty drama."

Laura leaned back in her chair, listening to the conversation around her. On top of being handsome and gorgeous and sexy, Hayden was also a nice guy, as the incident with Higgins demonstrated. A nice guy who was clearly not interested in pursuing her any further.

"So, Laura," Ellie interrupted her thoughts. "I've heard Tanner Olsen's truck was in front of your house—you are a busy girl, it seems." She laughed.

Laura blinked. To be honest, she'd already forgotten all about Tanner and the date she had with him on Friday. "I'm not even going to ask how you know," she said. "My colleague, Maria, has warned me about small towns, but I hadn't expected this intense scrutiny of my life."

"Carol Bingley." Arlene chuckled. "But she grows on you."

"Tanner is making extra cabinets for the kitchen—" Laura began.

"And taking her to Rocco's on Friday evening," Arlene interrupted her.

"So what about you, Ellie?" asked Annie. "You're so beautiful. I can't believe you're still single."

Ellie avoided their eyes as she always did when anyone asked her about dating or relationships. "Let's just say my experience with the opposite gender has been…really bad. It's not something I'll ever try again. I'm very happy all on my own. What I do need, though, are a few cats."

"I'm positive Cooper can help you," Willow said. "If I'm not mistaken, two stray ones have found their way to him during the past week."

"Will you ask him, please?" Ellie said.

Surprised, Laura caught Willow's eye. The cool and collected Ellie she'd come to know became agitated the moment she spoke about men.

Everybody had a story, a past hurt they were carrying around. She hoped at some point she'd be able to help Ellie with whatever hers was.

Chapter Fifteen

BY THE TIME Tim Higgins and Sheryl, his wife, drove away from the Weston ranch in their truck late Friday morning, Hayden felt drained. He hated any kind of confrontation.

Despite Higgins's objections, Hayden had insisted, though, that he and his family met with both Tim and his wife. It was time to get to the bottom of Tim's troubles and find a way to help their neighbor get his life back on track.

Becket hadn't been impressed, but both Willow and Cooper had agreed with Hayden's idea.

An angry and defiant Tim had arrived earlier this morning with his wife. He'd made it abundantly clear he'd only agreed to the meeting to please his wife. He had apologized for hurting Jessie, even though it was only after a nudge from his wife.

With photos Becket had taken using a drone over the last six months, they were able to show Tim their cattle had never been near his land. What the photos also showed clearly was how poorly Higgins Valley looked in comparison with the Weston Ranch and the other surrounding ranches.

They'd explained the concept of high-density grazing again, and Tim's wife seemed to understand what it was all about. Tim was still frowning when they left, but he had agreed to let them demonstrate again what they were doing as soon as summer arrived. They'd also offered to share some of their surplus hay with Higgins for the remainder of the winter.

Luke and Jessie came running out of the barn as Tim drove away. Hayden's heart just about jumped out of his body, and he was moving even before Luke skidded to a halt and bent to pick up Jessie. The truck stopped, and both Tim and his wife got out.

"Look, I'm…sorry about…about…" Tim was stuttering.

"The dog," his wife prompted.

"The dog," Tim repeated.

"And that you were frightened," Sheryl said.

"I'm sorry," Tim said.

Hayden put his hand on Luke's shoulder. "Thank you," he said.

"You really hurt Jessie," Luke said.

"I was angry. Sorry."

"It's okay, Mr. Higgins. Cooper and the vet helped Jessie, and Dad took me to Doctor Vivian."

Tim's wife looked at Hayden. "Please send us the bills."

"It's fine," he smiled. "We'll hopefully get the hay to you by Monday."

Sheryl's eyes were bright with tears. "You're a good man,

Hayden Weston. Your daddy would've been proud of you."

Luke waited until the truck had driven away before he put Jessie down. "Come on, Jessie. I'm hungry." Barking, Jessie followed him as they ran toward the house.

The vet had agreed Jessie was fine. How much it had to do with what the vet had given her or whether it had been Cooper's hands on the dog, he'd probably never know. He'd seen his brother with animals enough times to know he was the main reason Jessie was running around, keeping Luke happy. What exactly it was that his brother did, he didn't know, and he didn't ask.

"Glad that's done," Willow was saying as Hayden joined his siblings again. "So, what are you doing tonight?"

He shrugged. "Luke and I will probably watch a movie and—"

"Luke is spending the night with his friend Jonas, remember?" Willow interrupted him. "Why don't you join Coop, Becket, and me for a pizza at Rocco's after you've dropped Luke and Jessie off? Although nobody in this family seems to be dating at the moment, we can still have a meal in town now and again. It also gives Isabella a free night."

It was on the tip of his tongue to refuse when Willow mentioned Isabella.

Shaking his head, he put an arm around his sister's shoulders. "You know just how to get your way, don't you?"

Having pizza with his siblings in town sounded infinitely better than staring at the walls of his bedroom, thinking about Laura.

THERE WERE QUITE a few cars in front of Rocco's when Laura and Tanner arrived at the restaurant. As they neared the front door, Laura noticed Cooper's truck out of the corner of his eye. Her heart lurched and her breath hitched. Trying to ignore the silly signs, she smiled at Tanner as he opened the door and waited for her to step inside. Cooper's truck parked here didn't also mean Hayden would be here.

Rocco, or whoever had been responsible for the interior of the place, had obviously gone all out to replicate an Italian feel. The walls were covered with paintings of Tuscan landscapes, fountains, and statues. On the ceiling was a trellis with wines and oversized red grapes. All the tables were covered with red-and-white-checkered tablecloths. A red candle in an empty Chianti bottle was the final touch to help create a warm and charming atmosphere.

As they followed the waiter to their table, they were both greeted from all sides. She recognized several people, but thank goodness, there was no sign of the Westons. Tanner was obviously well-liked, and he smiled and nodded. They had to stop several times when someone got up to talk to him. It took a while before they reached their table.

He pulled out her chair. "Sorry about that. You've probably discovered everyone knows everyone in this town. And, by tomorrow, they will all be wondering about us."

She looked up quickly. "Tanner…this is…I mean…"

Smiling, he sat down. "Don't worry. Everyone in town knows you don't date anyone more than once."

Stunned, she stared at him. "Seriously? People are talking about my dating?"

"Of course. They talk about everyone. So, what can I get you to drink?"

Tanner was sweet and considerate, one of the good guys. He asked about her background and she asked him about his work. They were having a great time when something made her turn her head, and she locked gazes with Hayden Weston. Her heart shuddered to a halt.

The Westons sat at a table on the opposite side of the restaurant. That was why she hadn't seen them as they'd entered. Exhaling slowly, she put her hand on her tummy where the butterflies had woken up and were frolicking exuberantly, leaving her breathless.

Fortunately, at that point the waiter arrived with their food and blocked Hayden from her view. Catching her breath, she thanked the waiter and smiled at Tanner as they began to eat. The food looked great, but she didn't taste a thing. Her whole being was on high alert, aware of every single movement Hayden made, even though he was sitting at another table.

It had been three weeks since he'd last kissed her, but she could still recall every single sensation she'd experienced in his arms. Seriously, how long was this feeling going to last?

Tanner probably noticed she was staring at someone. He also turned his head. "Have you met Arlene's kids?" he asked.

She nodded. "Luke is in my class. We've met."

"Becket and I went to school together, so I've been on their ranch a few times. They're good people. I've heard Tim Higgins wanted to set their barn on fire and nearly killed his little boy, but instead of pressing charges, Hayden offered to help him."

Her eyes widened. The speed at which news spread in this town was astounding. "So everyone in town knows about it?"

Grinning, Tanner nodded. "Oh, yes. Carol Bingley and her friend, Betty, who works at the police dispatch, made sure of that."

Laura swallowed against the sudden lump in her throat. Hayden was so exactly the kind of man she could fall for—sexy and nice—making it all the harder to forget about him.

"So, Becket and Coop," Willow said. "How come you two aren't dating?"

As he struggled to keep breathing, Hayden tried to focus on the conversation. It was difficult. His gaze kept straying toward the table where Laura sat with Tanner Olsen. She looked beautiful. In a soft yellow top, her hair taken up, leaving her long neck bare, she was simply gorgeous.

It was clear she was having a great time. She hadn't stopped smiling at her date. He knew Tanner Olsen. A nice guy. He should be happy for Laura. Tanner would treat her well.

Cooper shrugged. "Having dinner with someone who doesn't really eat, who takes pictures of everything to post on social media, and who can't talk about anything other than herself, is exhausting. I prefer to stay at home with the animals. They're much more fun."

Willow laughed. "Okay, that's a valid excuse. What about you, Becket? What do you do with yourself when you don't date? I see you scribbling in a little notebook every now and again. Have you taken up drawing again? I still have the cards you made me when we were still at school. They're gorgeous."

Shrugging, Becket took a swig from his beer. "I'm taking a break from dating for the moment. Yeah, sometimes I still scribble."

Willow angled her head. "What you do is way more that scribble, and you know it. Why don't you let me—?"

Becket shook his head. "We're supposed to be having fun. Stop asking so many questions."

"Sorry." She grinned, clearly without any remorse. Her blue eyes turned toward Hayden. "You haven't stopped looking at Laura since she and Tanner Olsen walked in. You obviously have a thing for her. Why don't you do something about it?"

Becket also turned to look in Laura's direction. "Word is Olsen's looking for a wife. He wants to settle down, have kids. Laura is a good choice."

A few ranchers they knew came over with beers, and Co-op and Becket got up to talk to them. Hayden nodded in their direction, but stayed seated. He didn't want to talk to anyone.

Willow leaned closer. "I wish you'd listen to your heart. You want to be with her. Anybody can see that."

Shaking his head, he crossed his arms. "I've had my turn—"

"Yes, you have," Willow interrupted him. "But there is nothing that says you can't be happy again."

Rubbing his face, he sighed. "How can I be happy again when…when Walker won't ever experience the joy of loving someone? And I'm the reason he's not around."

Willow frowned. "How can you say that? If anyone is to blame, it's me. I'm the one—"

"I was driving, Sis. And then there's Madeline. What about the promises I made when I married her?"

Sighing, Willow moved back. "You're looking for excuses because you're scared of getting hurt again. I understand that. Why don't you talk to Maddie and Walker? Tell them what you're feeling?"

Hayden glared at his sister. "In case you've forgotten,

they can't hear me. They're dead."

"Just because they're not here doesn't mean you can't talk to them," Willow said as Cooper and Becket sat down again.

Hayden finished his beer. His plate was also empty, so he could go home. Not that he'd really tasted anything. "I'm heading back. You'll drive safely?"

Cooper nodded.

TANNER ESCORTED LAURA right up to her front door.

"Thank you for a lovely night. I've really enjoyed it."

"Thank you for joining me. I should be finished with the cupboards by next Friday and can bring them on Saturday if it suits you? If there's enough time, I can also paint the wall."

"That sounds perfect, thanks. School starts on Monday, but I'm usually at home on a Saturday."

Smiling, he briefly touched her arm before he turned around. "Good night."

"Good night!" she called before she opened the front door. From the direction of her bedroom came Molly's plaintive yelps.

On her way to the bedroom, she took off her coat and pulled the pins from her hair. Shaking out her head, she opened the door. Molly shot past her, barking joyously as she charged toward the front door.

"So, what happened?" Laura laughed as she kicked off her boots before she followed Molly to the front door.

Molly kept barking excitedly.

"Earlier, you didn't want Tanner to be here and now…"

Molly was scratching the front door, jumping up and down, and barking nonstop.

"Molly, what has gotten into you?" Laura rushed forward. "Why are you barking? Is someone—?"

A knock on her front door stopped her in the middle of her sentence. Had Tanner forgotten something?

She opened the door, and promptly lost her breath. Standing on her porch, looking haggard and gorgeous at the same time, was Hayden. With an excited yelp, Molly ran past her and jumped up against Hayden's legs. Her heart dropped. Something was wrong. Luke?

"Is Luke okay?"

"He's staying the night with a friend."

That was all the butterflies in her tummy needed to really go to town. "Oh."

"Tanner didn't stay?"

Unable to talk, she shook her head.

Chapter Sixteen

"I WANT TO come in," Hayden said above Molly's barking.

Watching him, Laura opened the door. Because he couldn't wait to step inside, because he ached for her with every fiber of his being, he put his hands on either side of the frame of the door. He had to be honest with her.

"Nothing has changed. I...can't promise you anything."

"So, why are you here?"

"You're all I think about. I ache for you."

Without a word, she pushed the door. He stepped inside and, picking up the excited dog, closed the door behind him. Molly tried to lick his face.

"Does she greet everyone like this?" he smiled, scratching Molly behind her ears.

"She somehow knew you were outside," Laura said. "She wasn't very friendly with Tanner."

"Good girl." He chuckled.

Laura took Molly from him. "Let me put her in her bed."

He left his jacket on a chair before he followed Laura,

mesmerized by her swaying hips and those long, long legs. By the time they got to the living room, he was struggling to breathe.

She put Molly down on her bed. "Can I get you anything?"

"No."

"So…" As she turned around, he was right behind her. Her soft gasp went straight to his groin.

With unsteady hands, he pulled her closer, dropped his head, and put his mouth against her neck, where a pulse was beating frantically. "If this is not what you want, I'll leave. It'll probably kill me, but…"

She slipped her arms around him, and for a moment, he held her close, breathing in her scent, breathing in her very being. What he'd done to deserve to be with her like this, he didn't know. He was just deeply grateful. "Finally," was the only thought running through his mind.

He lifted his head, cupped her face. "I'm really here, with you," he whispered before his mouth found hers. Her lips were soft and warm, and within seconds, he was struggling to hold on to the reins of his self-control. He tried to focus instead on giving her as much pleasure as he could, but she opened her mouth. Hungry tongues met and he was lost.

Urgently, she moved against him, hooking one of those long limbs around his leg. Without taking his mouth from hers, he picked her up. Sliding her arms around his neck, she held on tightly as he staggered toward her room.

Only one bedside light was on, leaving the room full of shadows. Lifting his head, he let her slide down against his body.

"You feel what you do to me?" he whispered.

Nodding, those blue eyes nearly black with passion, she pulled his shirt from his jeans. With a soft smile, she opened the top button, and then the next. By the time she spread his shirt and put her mouth against his feverish skin, she'd destroyed any hope he'd had of staying in control. "Laura…"

He quickly got rid of his shirt before he kissed her again. As her mouth slid and angled under his, he ran his hands over her. It was to torture her, but he was also driving himself mad with want. As his hands slid underneath her top, he swallowed her moan.

Petals. Satin. Roses. And hot. So, so hot. Lifting his head, the back of his hand skimmed her breasts. "I have to see you."

With heavy eyelids, she lifted her arms. He swore he could hear his heart falling to the floor and shattering into a million pieces as he pulled the top over her head. In only a pale-pink bra cupping her gorgeous breasts, she nearly brought him to his knees.

With their gazes locked, he unhooked the clasp at the back. Finally, he could look his fill. "Beautiful. So, so beautiful," he murmured before his mouth closed around one hard nipple. Her soft moan slid right through him, sending his blood way beyond the boiling point.

Keeping one arm around her back, he suckled and nibbled and worshipped her breasts until her legs, or it could have been his own, gave way and they fell backwards on the bed.

Lifting herself on her elbow, she smiled at him. "Look at us, naked, on my bed."

He laughed. He wouldn't have thought he could laugh at a time like this, but she made it so easy. "Not quite." He lifted himself to get rid of his jeans.

Her eyes followed his every movement, widened. "No briefs?"

Kicking the jeans away, he turned onto her. "It's been a problem lately. Since a certain long-legged teacher arrived in town, to be precise." With great concentration, he stroked her shoulder and slid his hand down to her soft breasts. Cupping one, he couldn't resist another taste.

With a groan, she cradled his head as he feasted on her lushness.

LAURA WAS SWIMMING in a sea of pleasure. Hayden's mouth was driving her up and up a steep mountain while wave after wave of the most exquisite pleasure she'd ever experienced washed over her.

What the man could do with his hands and mouth was unimaginable. And the heat… She was past agonizing; she'd burst into flames. At this point, she would welcome any kind of release. Not even in her wildest dreams—and there were seriously X-rated ones—could she have conjured up a lover as attentive, as enthusiastic, and as deft as Hayden was turning out to be.

Somehow, he knew exactly where to touch her, how to send her blood roaring, how to push her heart into the next gear. Every stroke of his hands moved her closer and closer to the edge. Restlessly, she moved beneath his onslaught. There was still more. She could feel it and she didn't want to wait a second longer.

And as if he could read her mind, he flipped open the button of her jeans and, with her frantic help, got rid of them.

"Look at you," he murmured, swiping his hand from her breasts down over her body to where she was aching, throbbing, for him. "Beautiful, so, so beautiful…"

"Hayden…" she got out brokenly and pulled him close.

As his mouth closed over hers, his hand found her core. She'd waited so long for this, she'd been so ready for him for such a long time, his touch sent her right over the edge. Choking out his name, her fingers in his hair, she came undone.

When she opened her eyes, he'd put protection on and was above her, his eyes nearly black with need. For her. Feeling like the most beautiful woman on the planet, she opened her arms and welcomed him home.

"I want to give you more…" With a groan he slid into her.

Still struggling to breathe, she pulled him closer. "Let's fly together," she whispered against his lips before his mouth closed over hers.

He moved, slowly. Her body, so attuned to his every need, found his rhythm.

"Laura…" he breathed in her ear.

"Yeah?"

"Just. Laura," he murmured, as he increased the tempo.

Closing her eyes, she wrapped herself around him as they rode out the storm. All she could hear as she let herself be swept away was their ragged breathing, and all she could feel was the unspeakable pleasure of being here with him, making love.

Just when she thought she couldn't possibly handle more, she opened her eyes to find his amber ones, like liquid chocolate, focusing on her, egging her on to go faster, to give more, to love more.

Bending down, his mouth crushed down on hers. Behind her eyes, stars exploded, and together, they broke free.

HE HAD JUST enough energy to gather her in his arms and roll onto his back so that she was on top of him. In awe, he cradled her close, as they both tried to get their labored breathing under control.

"You okay?" he asked when he could finally speak.

Lifting her head, those blue eyes, desire still lurking in the depths, found his. Smiling, she nodded. "You?"

"That was…I've never…you're amazing." Rolling onto his side so that she was lying next to him, he looked down at her. "Tell me this is real. Tell me I'm not dreaming again?"

Stroking his back, she smiled. "This is as real as it gets. We're naked and in bed—"

"Naked and in your bed," he agreed. "To see the way you react when I touch you…I've never seen anything more beautiful."

Those soft hands had glided to the front. When she found him ready for her again, her eyes widened. "Really?"

"I've been ready since I saw you in Grey's Saloon." He chuckled as he bent down to kiss her.

THE TOUCH OF Hayden's hand against her cheek woke Laura. He was standing next to her bed, fully clothed. It was still dark outside.

"What time is it?" She sat upright, not bothering to pull up the sheet. He'd seen all there was to see.

"Five o'clock," he muttered, his eyes on her breasts. "I have to go."

"You sure?" she asked, licking her lips.

With a groan, he kissed her, his one hand cupping her breast. And just like that, the embers of last night's fire ignited again. She pulled him down. With a low, guttural sound, he surrendered.

It was close to six o'clock when he finally left. With Molly in her arms, Laura leaned against the door as Hayden jogged down the stairs. When he reached the sidewalk, he looked over his shoulder again.

Smiling, she blew him a kiss. He smiled—wide and happy. Her heart sighed. They hadn't talked again. There was nothing more to say. He'd said nothing had changed, but she wanted him, anyway.

After closing the front door behind her, she walked toward the kitchen with Molly still in her arms. "Well, Molly," she said, as she put the dog on the floor. "I suppose I'm actually having an affair with the cowboy."

The distant ache she'd probably always carry in her heart, she was going to ignore for the moment. Soon, when he left for the last time, there would be enough time for pain and tears.

WITHOUT CONSCIOUS THOUGHT, Hayden ended up at the graveyard. The sun wasn't up yet, but the pinkish light behind the mountains was already announcing the new day.

Slowly, he walked toward the last two graves—his wife's

and his brother's. For long moments, he stood there, drinking in the silence. It was bitterly cold, but he was only vaguely aware of the temperature.

"Willow said I should talk to you two," he finally said. Closing his eyes for a moment, he waited…for something. They didn't have to be alive to hear him, Willow had said. Blinking, he first moved to his brother's grave and put a hand on the cold stone.

He waited for the pain to slash his heart, the guilt to steal his breath. Long minutes passed as he stood there remembering his brother. A picture of Walker as he would always remember him flashed before him—laughing, joking with his siblings.

After a long time, he opened his eyes in wonder. There were no thoughts of pain or guilt. Grief still lingered. It probably always would. Not as sharp-edged as it had always been, but a dull ache, reminding him of how much joy Walker spread wherever he went.

Deep in thought, he moved to Madeline's grave. She'd been his first love, his first kiss, his first everything. "I'll always love you, Mads," he muttered. Not bothering to wipe away the tears, he crouched down. "I have something to tell you, though…"

When he drove away from the graveyard nearly two hours later, he was feeling lighter. It wasn't as if he was bringing home a new bride…the truck steered dangerously toward the one side of the dirt road. Cussing, he brought it back just before it hit the bushes.

Where did that come from? He'd been very clear with Laura—he couldn't give her anything permanent and she'd invited him into her house, into her bed, and into her arms, anyway.

A vivid image of Laura in a wedding dress, smiling at him, was suddenly just there—front and center in his mind. Cussing, he stopped and got out. Inhaling the cold air, he tried to clear his mind. He wanted to be with her, not...

Marry her? Have her around all the time? Be with her every night? Images of their entwined limbs from the night before had him just about hyperventilating. He leaned against his truck, trying to get his breathing under control.

Getting married wasn't on the table. Laura knew that. She accepted that. They'd be together until...

Yeah? The taunting little voice was back.

Upset and confused by his wayward thoughts, he got back in his truck and drove home. A fling, that was all this was. There was no future. It was temporary. At least until this mad need for her had receded.

As he parked in front of the homestead, he called his mother. It would be nice to have Laura at the family lunch tomorrow.

"Good morning, Hayden. When I saw your truck in front of Laura's house this morning, I was hoping you'd stop by for a coffee," she said before he could say hello.

So she'd seen the truck. He was still trying to think what

to say when she continued. "Shall I invite her for lunch for tomorrow, then?"

"Thank you, Mom, but please…"

"I know. You don't want to get married again. You should think about that, though. You still have your whole life in front of you. It's an awful long time to be alone. And what happens when someone else offers Laura a ring and a happily-ever-after? Have you picked up Luke yet?"

His head was spinning. Trust his mother to change subjects so rapidly. "No, he's staying till lunchtime."

"Why don't I pick him up and he can stay with me tonight? He hasn't been to visit his grandma in a while."

Maybe a good idea. It would give him time to clear his head. "Thanks, Mom. I'll come early."

"Of course you will. See you tomorrow!"

Cussing a blue streak, he got out of the truck just as Willow came out of his house. "There you are. I've made coffee. You didn't come home last night?" Her eyes were twinkling.

Hayden sighed. "Don't tell me the damn gossip mill has been at it again."

"Not that I've seen. Depends on where you've parked your truck, of course. You've been with Laura?"

He nodded. Everybody had probably seen his truck.

"And you've talked to Madeline and Walker?"

Of course she would know. "Yeah, I have."

"You're happy with Laura?"

"Yeah, but it's…"

"Temporary?" Shaking her head, she touched his shoulder. "Listen to your heart, Hayden. Listen to your heart." With a wave, she walked toward her truck.

The house was empty. Silent. It was strange not to have to worry about Luke today. His phone was in his hand before he thought too much about it. There were chores that had to be done, but he'd be free this afternoon.

Chapter Seventeen

SUNDAY LUNCH WITH Arlene and her family was pure torture. Of course, it was lovely to see everyone, but by the time they'd finished dessert, Laura was convinced she'd burst into flames at any minute.

Molly was happy to sit on Cooper's lap. Laura had wanted to leave her in the kitchen, but was assured they were used to animals sitting with Cooper during meals.

Luke was on her right, chatting nonstop about his visit to his friend yesterday, but it was the heat radiating from the body on her other side that was wreaking havoc with her senses. Hayden's earthy, musky scent was enough to send her blood rushing through her veins. He also kept finding reasons to touch her, reminding her of the two nights she'd spent in his arms. She was ready to explode.

Yesterday morning, she'd still been pacing her kitchen, trying to figure out how having a fling was supposed to work, when Hayden had called again. He'd picked her up around lunchtime and she'd spent the rest of the day and night with him.

It was bittersweet. They'd hardly slept. Hayden had unleashed a wild woman, one she barely recognized. Up until now she'd never thought of herself as very sensual, but when she was with him she'd discovered feelings and emotions she'd never felt before.

They wouldn't often be able to be together, she knew that. Both she and Hayden worked during the day, and in the evenings, he had a son to look after. She also couldn't stay with Hayden when Luke was home. Nobody needed to tell her that. It would complicate things even more.

Being so close to him, but unable to touch him freely, was getting more difficult by the minute. The smirks on everyone's faces weren't helping, either.

A quick look around the table assured her everyone had finished eating. She got up, picking up her plate and Luke's. "Thanks, Arlene. I'm doing the dishes today."

"I knew there was a reason I liked you." Becket grinned as he got up with his own plate.

"Nonsense, you're our guest," Arlene tried, but Laura just smiled.

"I'll help Miss Anderson," Luke called out.

"We'll both help," Hayden said, as he also got up.

Everyone ended up in the kitchen, Molly still happy in Cooper's arms. While Laura rinsed the dishes, Hayden stacked them in the dishwasher. He made sure his fingers touched hers every single time. Inhaling deeply, she tried to concentrate on the task at hand.

"So, Hayden, what exactly is going on between you and

Laura?" asked Cooper, scratching Molly's ears.

Laura's breath caught in her throat. Oh, dear. She didn't dare look in Hayden's direction.

"Dad likes her," Luke said.

"Laura, what about you?" Becket asked.

"Okay, you two, that's enough," Hayden said as he closed the washing machine. Taking Laura's hand, he turned to look at the rest of his family. "I'm taking Laura home. Luke, will you please stay here with Grandma until I'm back? Mom?"

"Of course, he can stay and so can Molly." Arlene smiled, holding out her hand toward Luke. "Come on. I've bought new books. I'm so happy you've discovered reading..." They disappeared around the corner.

"Take your time," Willow said. "I'll take Luke home with me and stay with him until you're back."

"Thanks, I appreciate that," Hayden said as he took Laura's elbow and steered her toward the front door. He handed her jacket to her and put his on.

"We haven't finished the dishes," she said while slipping into her jacket.

"Don't worry about that." He'd opened the door, and grabbing her hand, he pulled her after him. Without talking, he walked in the direction of her house with such long strides, she had a hard time keeping up.

By the time they got to her house, they were both breathing hard. Without asking, Hayden unlocked the front door, steered her inside, and kicked it closed.

Before his jacket hit the ground, he was pushing her against the wall. She tried to catch her breath, but his mouth found hers in a searing kiss, rekindling last night's embers. Within seconds, she was burning up. Without breaking the kiss, she shrugged out of her jacket before slipping her arms around his neck.

Reveling in the taut muscles beneath her fingers and the stubble of his beard against her face, she melted against him.

This was what she'd been waiting for the whole day. This was what she'd been craving—being like this, with him. How was she ever going to let this cowboy go?

USUALLY HAYDEN HAD a lot of self-control, but around this gorgeous creature he didn't stand a chance. He wanted her with a fever that had been burning inside of him since he'd dropped her off at her house earlier this morning.

His hands had found their way beneath the soft blue top she was wearing. Desperate to touch her soft curves, his fingers slipped beneath her bra. His whole body ached for her, but he also wanted to spend time kissing her. It was all he'd had on his mind all day.

Angling his head, he deepened the kiss and their tongues met, mingling with their groans. He loved how she leaned into him. But it wasn't enough. Not nearly.

He pulled his shirt over his head. As he dropped it on the floor, Laura's top joined his. She was leaning back against the wall, her eyes dark pools of blue ink, her breath coming through her lips in gasps. A fist of desire hit him in the gut, the force so intense, it nearly knocked him to his knees. Beautiful. So, so beautiful. Today, an ink-blue bra covered her gorgeous breasts.

"Laura," he breathed, as he bent down to taste her while he ran his hands over her hot flesh. Her hardened nipples against his mouth were so erotic, he struggled not to lose control. Her moan reverberated right through her body while she stroked and loved his body with her soft hands. He was ready to explode. The waiting was over.

With his blood racing through his veins, he lifted his head. "I want you. Right now, right here."

With her eyes never leaving his, she shimmied out of her jeans, while he kicked his to the side as well. His eyes dropped to her satiny legs. "These"—he lifted her one leg against his hip—"these are the holy grail," he muttered before he caught her mouth again.

To be here with her like this, steeped in her scent, driven to the brink of madness by her soft skin, the satiny texture of her hair around his face, had seemed impossible. His need for her was more intense than anything he'd ever experienced.

Catching her mouth with his again, he slipped his hand down her body to her core. She was ready for him. And then he couldn't wait another second. The need to be one with her was so intense, so overwhelming, nothing else mattered.

With a cry, he entered her, and only when she clamped around him like a velvet glove did the chaos inside him settle. Both her legs wrapped around him, pulling him closer. For a second, they held one another, their breathing labored, his muscles straining. And then, completely in sync, they began to move.

Not wanting to miss a thing, he watched her, trying not to let the red mist blur his vision. In awe, he watched her flushed face, her eyes dark and stormy, and her hair tangled in his fingers.

Inside him, something moved, struggling to break free. Something had changed, but pushing the thought aside, he focused on giving the woman in his arms as much pleasure as he could. Wave after wave of sensation broke over them and together, they crested.

IT WAS EARLY evening when Hayden left. With her lips still tingling from his last kiss, Laura closed the front door and walked back to her room. Molly was still at Arlene's, but before she could fetch the dog, she had to get dressed.

Dreamily, she walked back to her room. Oh, my. The bed was still rumpled and one pillow had ended up on the floor. Picking it up, she pressed her face into it. All Hayden.

A groan escaped. How was she supposed to fall asleep tonight?

What the man could do with his hands and mouth... Blushing, she touched her warm cheeks. She'd never felt so beautiful, so cherished, so loved before.

The room tilted, and she quickly sat down on the bed. Loved. For long minutes, she stared at the pillow in her hands. Loved. With a groan, she dropped her head in her hands. She'd gone and done exactly what she shouldn't have done—she'd fallen in love with the cowboy.

That was why she'd welcomed him into her bed so quickly. Her heart had known how she felt about him before she'd consciously realized it. She loved him. With every fiber of her being. Deeply, irrevocably, passionately.

He didn't feel the same, though. A fling, that was all that this was. Temporary, snatching moments together when possible.

The lump in her throat was sudden, unexpected. She swallowed the sob that was about to slip out. Jumping up, she blinked a few times and cleared her throat. It was no use crying over something she couldn't change or stop. That was something she'd learned the hard way when her mom had fallen ill.

Happily-ever-after was a myth, after all. She knew that. Not even her beautiful mother had one. Yes, she'd married the love of her life, but then an illness nobody could have predicted had taken over her body. There hadn't been a cure.

Grabbing her jeans, she quickly slipped them on. At least she had a dog who loved her unconditionally.

Minutes later, she crossed the lawn to Arlene's house. At the front door, she inhaled deeply and made sure her hair was in place. It was a bit disconcerting, knowing she was about to see the mother of the man with whom she'd made love for the last few hours.

Arlene was gracious, as always. Only the twinkle in her eye gave her away. "What about a cup of tea?" Arlene asked as Laura bent to pick up Molly.

"Thanks, Arlene, but I still have a few things to do for tomorrow's class. Thanks for keeping Molly. I hope she didn't make a mess?"

"Not at all. She fretted a bit when Cooper wanted to leave, but he did that thing he does with animals and she calmed down."

"That thing?" Laura asked. She'd picked up here and there about Willow's ability to just know things about her loved ones. Although she didn't understand it, she'd experienced the way Cooper was with animals herself when she was at his place for dinner and to pick up Molly.

Arlene smiled as she accompanied Laura down the footpath. "My mom was fey, as the Irish call the ability to have a foreboding when something bad is about to happen. Willow gets that from her. She also seems to know what other people feel. She can read their emotions, so to speak. That's one of the reasons she prefers to live on the ranch." Arlene chuckled. "That and her preference to swim naked in the hot spring on the ranch. Cooper has it too, in a way, although I think he deliberately directs his instinct toward animals. Since Willow was a little girl, she'd know things about her brothers they'd rather not have anybody know. Used to make them so mad. And Coop...he has such a big heart, I worry about him sometimes. And you know what? I think our Luke has been blessed with the same thing. I've only recently become aware of that."

Surprised, Laura looked at her. "Really?"

"He knows how his dad feels about you. Hayden wouldn't have told him."

Laura swallowed. Arlene obviously knew what Laura and her son had been up to earlier in the day. She should tell her what was really going on. "Hayden and I...it's only temporary."

Arlene looked at her. "And how do you feel about that?"

Looking down at Molly, Laura swallowed. "I want to be with him for as long as he wants me."

"Because you love him?"

Laura inhaled sharply. "How...?" Too late, she realized she'd confessed her love for Hayden with that one word.

"Oh, sweetie," Arlene said, giving a quick hug. "They were all still struggling with Walker's death when Madeline became ill. Hayden never had time to really process his grief. He has Luke to look after. He's a protector and always has been. My oldest believes he must be strong all the time because that's the way to safety. He's been denying his own fears and weaknesses for so long, I don't even think he knows that. But when you're around, Laura, he's different. I can see something of the son I remember in his eyes. Don't give up on him too soon?"

Laura couldn't speak. Her throat was clogged up. Nodding, she returned Arlene's hug before she left.

She wasn't the one who was planning on giving up. Drama and complications—exactly what she hadn't wanted when she'd arrived in Marietta. But then, her heart had decided otherwise.

Chapter Eighteen

BY LATE FRIDAY afternoon, Hayden was restless, moody, irritated. Fed up with the whole situation, he got out of his truck. It had been a long day.

Frustration was a live thing, clawing at his insides. He hadn't seen Laura since Sunday. They'd texted and he'd phoned her every night, but there hadn't been a chance to be with her again. When he was free, she was teaching, and when she had free time, he had Luke with him.

Willow had been in Bozeman for the week to finalize the upcoming exhibition of her artwork, so he couldn't even ask her to babysit. Of course, there was always his mother, but he didn't feel comfortable asking her to look after his son while he had sex with her neighbor.

With his hand on the front door, he froze. Sex? What happened when he was with Laura was not just sex. That had become crystal clear over the past week. Something so much more was at play when he was with her. They connected on a level much deeper than he'd ever experienced before, one that instinctively guided him to give her what she needed, made it clear what she liked, what made her fly—that had never happened before.

Just the thought of her cresting over and over when they were together was enough to send his blood roaring through his body.

Inhaling deeply, he rubbed his face. How could he feel this way? Wasn't he betraying what he and Madeline had?

As he opened the front door, Willow's truck stopped behind him.

He turned around to welcome her. "How was your week?" he asked as she got out of her car.

Giving him a once-over, she angled her head. "I had a great week, thanks. Something tells me you're not so happy, though."

"It's been a difficult week. Laura and I have both been so busy. Can you stay with Luke for a while? I want to fetch Laura. I'm hoping she'll come to the ranch for the weekend."

Willow laughed. "You've got it bad, don't you?"

He couldn't stop the grin even if he tried. "I must go. Thanks, Sis," he called out, already on his way to his truck.

By the time he reached the outskirts of Marietta, he was on fire. He'd had to force himself not to drive too fast. In a few minutes, he was going to see her, touch her, and make love to her.

Make love to her. Love. Something inside him that had been trying to escape for weeks now finally struggled free. He slowed down and stopped the truck. Of course he loved her. He probably had since that very first moment she'd opened her class door. And he also remembered the exact moment his heart had acknowledged it—when she'd lifted her arms so that he could pull her top over her head.

With his heart lighter and a stupid grin on his face, he started his truck again. Surely she felt the same way? He stepped on the gas. The urgency to be with her, to hold her, and to tell her how he felt was rushing through his veins.

LAURA QUICKLY PUT the very unhappy Molly in her room and closed the door before she jogged toward the front door. Tanner had texted earlier while she was still at school. He'd finished the kitchen cabinets and could bring them during the afternoon—apparently, he had extra help that would make transporting the cabinets easier.

It had been a frustrating week. She missed Hayden something fierce. They'd texted and he'd phoned every night, but she wanted to be with him and touch him, not just talk to him on the phone, damn it. Hayden had Luke to consider, but there wasn't anything that said she couldn't go to him. It was the weekend, after all.

Smiling, she opened the door. Just the thought that she'd see Hayden soon had her just about dancing. Tanner and another man were standing on her porch with the cabinets.

Tanner introduced her to his friend. "If you're thinking of asking, I must warn you, though. You only get one date with this lady," Tanner teased.

Laughing, she opened the door wider. "This town and the gossip! I don't understand why everyone is so interested in my dating habits. Come on in, thanks."

It didn't take them long, and within fifteen minutes they were on their way. Tanner was willing to come back tomorrow to paint the wall, but she had other plans. Painting a wall was something she could do on her own, anyway.

With a still-barking Molly in her arms, Laura took a minute to admire the beautiful cabinets. Tanner had painted them in a dove's egg blue paint—she loved the look.

"Oh, shush." She laughed and scratched Molly behind the ears. "They're gone. Look at my pretty cupboards!"

Molly was still seriously indignant about the strangers who'd been in her house, though, and gave a few more yelps before she quieted down. "There we go…" Laura crooned as she walked toward her bedroom. "Let me quickly grab a few things. Then we can go."

She put Molly on her bed and put a few necessary items in her bag. It was nearly half past five and the sun had already set. Hopefully, she could reach the ranch before it was completely dark.

FEELING BETRAYED, HAYDEN parked in front of the homestead and got out of his truck. He was angry, hurt, and frustrated. Well, he'd wanted to know whether Laura felt the same way and now he knew. She obviously didn't.

For a moment, he wanted to get back in his truck and just keep driving. With a sigh, he entered the house. His family would know something was wrong. He didn't even need to pretend to be okay.

From the direction of Luke's room, he could hear Jessie barking. Everyone else was in the living room, drinking beer, when he entered.

Willow frowned. "Where's Laura?"

Trying to get his breath under control, he threw up his hand.

"Hayden?" Willow got up. "What's wrong?"

"Aren't you supposed to know these things?" he barked and immediately felt like an idiot. "Sorry…I'm…sorry. Laura is at home. With Tanner Olsen."

Willow's eyes widened. "Surely, you're mistaken—"

"I was there. I saw his truck. I saw him entering her house!" He only realized how loudly he was talking when Luke came running into the living room and hid behind Willow. "I'm sorry for yelling, Luke. You haven't done anything. Come here."

Reluctantly, Luke walked closer to him. "Are you angry with Miss Anderson? 'Cos she likes you too."

Fortunately, Becket handed him a beer and he didn't have to answer. He couldn't sit down. Different motions and feelings were churning inside him, driving him nuts. There was something he was supposed to grasp, but it stayed just out of his reach.

"Hayden!" Willow's voice penetrated his muddled thoughts.

He stopped and stared at her. Something was wrong. By this time, he could read Willow's face. Something had happened. "What?"

"Laura…" Willow said. "Her car…she's in a ditch, a few miles from our gate."

"Isabella!" Hayden yelled, as they all sprinted toward the door. "Watch Luke for me, please?"

FOR A FEW minutes, Laura couldn't move. She was breathing and she could feel her toes, so she was okay. The car, maybe not.

Molly's yelp brought her out of her shock. Poor Molly crawled toward her from the back seat. A sob escaped, and Laura picked up the trembling dog. "Oh, sweetie." Cradling Molly close to her, Laura started shivering. "Oh, my goodness, Molly. I didn't want to hit the elk. That's why I swerved, but I didn't know we'd end up in a ditch in the middle of nowhere."

It was dark outside, the cold slowly seeping into the car. "Let's see if we can get out of here…" She was shaking so much, it took a few tries to turn the key, but there was just nothing. Again, she tried. Still nothing.

"Well, Molly, we can sit here and cry, or we can do something about this. We can't be too far away from the ranch. Well, I hope not. Let's see, shall we?"

Hiking her bag over her shoulder and hugging Molly tightly, she tried to open the door. But it wouldn't budge.

Feeling close to tears, she opened her bag and found her phone. The surprise for Hayden was turning out to be a disaster.

She phoned Hayden. No ringtone. With a groan, she looked at her phone. Of course there wouldn't be a signal. Everything that could go wrong was going sideways simultaneously. A tear slipped out and rolled over her face. Whimpering, Molly cuddled closer to her.

Hugging the dog, she burst into tears and let her head drop on the steering wheel. All she'd wanted to do was to get to Hayden. The universe, it seemed, had other plans.

***

WITH HIS HEART beating like a runaway train, Hayden raced down the dirt road. What the hell was Laura doing out here? Where was Tanner-freaking-Olsen?

As he drove over a hill, he saw the red taillights of a car in a ditch next to the road. It was too dark to immediately see whether it was Laura's car, but as he stopped, the lights of the truck fell on the ditch. His breath left his body in one swoosh. It was her car.

He was out of his truck and running toward the red lights without conscious thought, his only need to get to Laura and make sure she was okay. Behind him was the sound of another vehicle stopping, but he kept going. It was probably his siblings in Willow's truck.

"Laura!" he shouted, as he scrambled down the side of the ditch. "Laura!"

A tearful face lifted from the steering wheel. Laura. Exhaling, he hurried closer. She was alive, and that was all that mattered now. The door wouldn't budge.

"Here, Hayden. This one is open!" Becket called from the passenger side of the truck, and, cussing, Hayden hurried around the car.

Becket's upper body was in the car and when he stepped back, he had Molly in his arms. "Thanks," Hayden muttered as he moved inside to help Laura.

She was shivering, her face pale in the lights of the truck. "What the hell are you doing out here?" he scolded as he picked her up. "You could've been killed!"

"Don't shout at me!" she cried before she burst into tears. She buried her face against his chest.

"I'm sorry. I was just so scared." He combed her hair out of her face and froze. "You're bleeding," he cried out. "Damn it, Laura…what happened?"

Cooper hurried closer. "Let me see."

Sniffing, Laura lifted her head. Cooper placed one hand

against her face. "It's going to be okay," he whispered, as he kept his hand against her temple.

"How did you know where to find me?" Laura hiccupped.

"Willow knew."

"You okay, sweetie?" Willow asked as Cooper stepped back.

Sniffing, Laura nodded. "I think so. There was an elk in the road. One minute, there was nothing and then this big thing suddenly just stood there."

Hayden's heart just about stopped. That was exactly what happened the night Walker died. "So, in your effort not to hit it, you ended up in a ditch?" Hayden yelled, his blood roaring in his ears.

Willow stroked his back. "It's okay. She's fine. Look, no more blood either."

His sister was right. The blood flow had stopped. Coop had done his thing—whatever it was—again.

"Sorry," he mumbled. "It's just…that's what happened the night Walker died. The elks roam all over in winter, looking for food. This kind of thing happens all too often."

"I'm sorry…"

"You reacted instinctively. Nothing to be sorry about," Willow said.

Cradling her close, he followed the others out of the ditch. "Do you need to see a doctor?"

Laura shook her head. "Molly and I just had a scare, but

we're okay. Where is she?"

"I've got her," said Coop. "She's okay."

"Thank you. Oh, I have a bag. It's still in the car."

"I'll get it," Willow offered. "There is a lovely hot meal waiting for us at home. Luke will be so happy to see his favorite teacher."

Minutes later, they were on the road again, driving back to the homestead. Hayden had one hand on the wheel and one hand laced with Laura's fingers. He knew she was with Tanner, but damn it, he simply had to touch her.

His heart hadn't quite settled yet. Talking wasn't possible right now. Now that his adrenaline had settled down, all the really bad scenarios were running through his mind. One of which in particular kept robbing him of his breath—she could've been killed.

As they stopped in front of the homestead minutes later, the front door flew open. Luke, with Jessie on his heels, ran toward them. "Miss Anderson…" he cried. "Is she okay?"

"She's fine. See for yourself." Hayden smiled as he climbed out of his truck.

Luke rushed to the passenger side and opened the door.

As Laura got out, he stepped closer and helped her. Luke hugged her legs. "You're here," he sighed.

Sniffing, she bent down and hugged him. "I'm okay. Really. Do you think there's enough food for me too?"

Luke took Laura's hand. "Yes, come on. Isabella always makes a lot."

Chapter Nineteen

HAYDEN WAS QUIET all through dinner. Everyone had had a scare, but there was something else going on. What it was, Laura wasn't sure, but Hayden was avoiding looking at her. Something had changed between them. Yes, he'd come to her rescue, and yes, he'd held her hand, but he hadn't said a word.

Her heart sank. He'd probably decided he was finished with the fling. She'd never had a fling before; she didn't know how it was supposed to work. Maybe a week was the appropriate timeline. How would she know? And she'd brought a bag, thinking she'd be welcome.

They'd all just finished eating, and Luke and Jessie had left the kitchen. Sounds of barking and a little boy's laughter came from the direction of the living room. Well, she couldn't stay here. She'd phone Maria, and hopefully, she could pick her up before she burst into tears again.

Before she could push her chair back, though, Willow cleared her throat. "So, Laura, you were driving out here to…?"

Oh, dear. Of course, Willow would ask the question. No

hiding from her. "I…um…I was on my way to see…to see Hayden. I thought we still had…" Taking a breath, she blurted out. "I wanted to see Hayden, but it's clear it was a mistake."

Frowning, Hayden met her eyes.

She got up. "You've obviously changed your mind about us. Excuse me. I'll call Maria."

Willow got up too. "You two"—she said, pointing to Hayden and Laura—"need to talk. Laura, just so you know, Hayden drove into town to fetch you earlier today, but he turned back when he saw another truck in front of your house. I'm taking Luke and Jessie home with me."

"I'll take Molly," Cooper said with a smile.

With a last wave from Willow, they trooped out of the kitchen.

Isabella had left earlier. Minutes after Hayden's family left, the house was quiet. He and Laura were still standing on opposites side of the table.

"You came into town to fetch me?" she finally asked.

"And saw Tanner entering your house."

Her eyes narrowed. "So why didn't you come in?"

"You had company."

Crossing her arms, she shook her head. "Tanner made freestanding cabinets for my kitchen. He was going to bring them tomorrow, but this afternoon he had help to transport them. That was why he was at my house, something you would've known if you've knocked on the door. Actually, you should've known it without having to ask. Damn it, Hayden. We've been together, I've given you my body, showed you how I feel about you, but…okay, I get it. You're finished with the fling. I just wish you would've told me." Turning around, she walked out of the kitchen.

Showed you how I feel about you—the words had knocked his breath from his body and it took him a few seconds to recover. "Laura!" he roared as he followed her with long strides.

She had her phone in her hand.

"How you feel about me?" He walked right up to where she was standing. "Why don't you tell me exactly how you feel about me?"

A tear slipped out of the corner of her one eye. Without bothering to wipe it away, she looked at him. "Why?"

Her eyes told him everything he wanted to know. Something that had been rolled up tightly inside him eased out slowly, and a warmth he'd forgotten about spread through his body, reaching even those parts that had been frozen for a long time. He didn't deserve a second chance at happiness and he didn't deserve love again, but here he was with Laura, and as impossible as he'd thought it to be, she was offering both.

Cupping her face, he wiped the tears away with his

thumbs. "Because I've just realized today something my heart has known since the moment I saw you in Grey's Saloon."

She stilled, even stopped breathing. Those blue eyes were looking straight into his very soul.

The smile that probably split his face in two came from deep inside of him. "It's complicated. I have things to sort out in my mind. I didn't expect this, didn't expect you, but I love you. And I want you to know, what I feel when I'm with you, I've never felt before."

Because he was standing so close to her, he could see the precise moment his words sank in. She exhaled slowly. "You love me?"

"I do."

"And?"

"And as soon as I know how you feel about me, we can talk about the 'and.'"

"You must know. I've showed you every time we were together."

"The words, Laura. I need to hear to the words."

"Of course I love you, you idiot." She sniffed. "Mind you, I didn't want to. Another guy with baggage, I thought, but then I fell for you, anyway. Can we now please kiss and get naked? It's been a long week."

With a laugh, he picked her up. "Yes, ma'am. I don't mind if we do."

As he strode to his room with Laura in his arms, his heart

finally settled. They had to talk. But first, he wanted to show her with his body how deep his feelings ran, how much she meant to him, and how extraordinary he thought she was.

Sunday morning, Laura opened her eyes slowly. She was alone. Luke's laughter floated up the stairs, followed by Jessie's barking. Faraway sounds from outside penetrated slowly.

Stretching her arms above her head, she smiled. After the past two nights she'd spent in Hayden's arms, she was aware of muscles she hadn't used before. What the man could do with his hands and mouth was just…wow. She'd fallen for an enthusiastic and ingenious lover. The thought of leaving him and Luke later today filled her with dread.

Luke had accepted her presence in the house without questions. She and Hayden should talk—with each other and, of course, with Luke. When they were alone together, however, talking was the last thing she thought about.

Hayden had things to work out in his mind, he'd said. How long that would take and what happened after this weekend, she didn't know. But in this moment, she was so happy.

When she'd moved to Marietta, the last thing she'd expected had been that she'd meet her person—that one guy whom she was meant to be with. She loved him as she hadn't known it was possible to love. Being with him, making love with him, filled her body, her soul, her whole being.

Marriage wasn't on the table. Hayden had been very clear about that from the start, but he loved her. That was all that mattered, anyway.

From outside came the sound of another truck, and she jumped up quickly. They were having lunch with Arlene. She'd better get dressed.

HAYDEN WAITED FOR Laura to finish breakfast. He'd deliberately not gone up to the room again. His mother was expecting them for lunch. When he was with her, he had to touch her and when he touched, he wanted her—all of her. Shaking his head, he grinned. He had it bad. Really bad.

They had to talk. And he knew where he wanted to have the talk. Willow had already left to go into town and had taken Luke and the dogs with her.

"All done?" he asked as he got up from the table.

"Yes, I'll quickly rinse this…"

"Just leave it. Before we go into town, will you come with me? By the way, the mechanic we usually use will tow it away and fix it for you. He's with the car and says it would probably be ready by the end of the week."

Frowning, she put her hands on her hips. "You didn't have to do that. I was going to phone tomorrow—"

He moved closer before she could finish her sentence. "Please let me do this for you? If I'd brought you home as I planned to do, your car wouldn't have been in a ditch."

Stiffly, she nodded. "Thank you. But I'm quite capable of fixing my own problems, okay?"

Catching her hands, he pulled her closer. "I know. It's one of the reasons I've fallen in love with you."

She was still frowning, though, and opened her mouth to say something again, but being this close to her, surrounded by her flowery scent, all he could think about was kissing her. His lips caught hers, and like every single time, he was lost.

Kissing Laura was fast becoming addictive. He loved the way her lips immediately softened and parted under his, how she melted against him, and how the curves of her body seemed to have been made to fit against his.

Slipping his hands under her top, he lifted his head. "Everything else will have to wait…" He pulled her top over her head.

Fortunately, the table had been cleared. It would have to do.

HALF AN HOUR later, they drove away from the homestead. Hayden had her hand tightly in his. Laura put her other hand on her tummy, where the butterflies hadn't quite settled yet. Her body was still singing, her blood still rushing through her veins. She loved this man something fierce.

She studied his face, his broad shoulders, his muscled legs, and, within minutes, she was so hot, she struggled to breathe. Inhaling deeply, she looked out of the window. She'd just straightened her clothes after being ravished on the kitchen table and here she was, ready to jump on him again.

Grinning, he squeezed her hand. "Am I forgiven?"

"This time," she said, lifting her chin. "I've been on my own for a while now and can handle my own problems."

"But now you have me to help you."

"But for how long?" slipped out before she could stop herself. "A fling means it's temporary and I can't—"

He stopped the truck so suddenly, if it hadn't been for the seat belt and Hayden's arm that had shot out to protect her, she would've fallen forward.

His eyes mere slits, Hayden glared at her. "I love you, damn it. We're way past a freaking fling."

"So what are we then, Hayden? This time, *I* need to hear the words."

He opened and closed his mouth a few times before he inhaled deeply. "That's what I want to talk to you about."

Her throat too clogged up to talk, Laura nodded.

Without another word, Hayden started his truck and drove further. Those stupid butterflies were going crazy. She didn't want to be excited, but the light in his eyes was making it difficult. Was it possible that they could…?

Closing her eyes, she tried to calm her breathing. She'd have to wait.

A few minutes later, they stopped under a huge tree. Right next to it, neatly fenced in with a white gate, was a graveyard. Hayden helped her down from the truck.

Lacing his fingers with hers, he opened the gate. "The family graveyard. These two here," he said as they walked past the first graves. "These are where our great-grandfather and great-grandmother lie. He tamed the land with her by his side. These two," he continued as they walked past the next two graves, "Are Grandpa's and my nana's. Dad lies here." He swallowed. "I still miss him every day. And this"—he pointed toward the next one—"this is Walker's grave, and here…" he said as walked to the last grave. "Lies Madeline."

For a long time, they just stood there, the cold slowly seeping through their clothes. A deep sadness filled Laura. Madeline had been so very young, it had to have been heartbreaking to leave her son and husband behind.

Finally, Hayden took her hand and they walked back to the truck.

The inside was nice and warm. Turning to her, Hayden pulled her into his arms. With a sigh, she leaned against him. For a while, he didn't say anything, just holding her tightly until their breathing slowed down.

Finally, he cleared his throat. "I don't know how this works. I don't know whether showing you my dead wife's grave is something one is supposed to do or not. I'm trusting my gut here. I loved her, we had a son together, and she will always be a part of me and Luke. I also wanted you to see Walker's grave. I'll probably always feel guilty about the night he died. I fell for you the moment I saw you, but I didn't think...I couldn't believe I deserved a second chance at love. It didn't seem fair that I wanted to marry again, and Walker would never have the chance to do that and to raise a family."

Marry again. Hayden was still talking, but after those two words, she didn't hear another word. She turned to face him.

He stopped mid-sentence before he rubbed his face. "I shouldn't have brought you here," he sighed. "I just thought..."

"You said 'marry again.'"

Frowning, he nodded. "Yes, I'm working up to that."

Happiness exploded inside her. "Why don't you just ask me?"

He looked puzzled. "Ask you what?"

"To marry you."

"You mean..."

"Ask me."

"I wanted to tell you about Walker and Madeline first, so that..."

"We'll get to that. Ask me."

The grin that lit up his face was a picture she would always carry in her heart. "I don't have a ring—"

"I don't need a ring right now."

Slowly, his smile faded. He took her hands in his. "I don't know how fair it is to ask you. I come with baggage, something you specifically mentioned you don't want—a son, a ranch, an interfering mother, a sister who knows things, a brother who talks to animals, and I worry about Becket. He isn't happy, and I'm not sure why. We have people who work for us, who are our responsibility. Right now, the ranch is doing well, but it could change at any minute. There's Madeline and Walker and…I don't even know whether you're going to like living out here—"

She put her hands around his face. "Ask me."

He stilled. Blue eyes watched her. Breathlessly, she waited.

"Laura," he finally said, his eyes suspiciously bright. "You told Molly something that stuck with me."

Surprised, she looked at him. "How do you know what I've told Molly? Don't tell met you're another Willow?"

"No." He smiled. "You called me without realizing it. So I heard what you said. When you fall in love, it would be with someone who wants to be with you, always. Well, I'm that guy. I can't believe that I've found you. I love you, and I want to be with you as long as we live. Will you marry me? And my baggage?"

Swallowing against the huge lump in her throat, she nodded. "Yes, Hayden. I will marry you. Any day, anywhere. But there is something I must tell you. I need to be honest with you…"

He stopped breathing.

"I fell in love with Luke long before I met you."

For another heartbeat, he stared at her before he pulled her close. "No wonder I'm besotted with you," he whispered brokenly in her ear.

Relaxing against him, she slipped her arms around him. "Tell me about Walker and Madeline."

THEY WERE VERY late for Sunday lunch. Everyone was still sitting around Arlene's table. When Luke saw them, he jumped up and ran toward them, Molly and Jessie on his heels. Thinking he was going to his father, Laura stepped aside, but the little boy's focus was on her, and he threw his arms around her legs.

Crouching down, she hugged him. "Have you left any food for us?"

"Grandma had to stop Becket from eating all the chicken," he whispered loudly.

As everyone laughed, they joined the others at the table. Luke pulled his chair close to Laura's before he sat down. Laura looked for Molly, but she was already sitting on Cooper's lap.

Willow was grinning from ear to ear, but for once, she didn't say anything.

The food was lovely, but Laura hardly tasted a thing. She was still walking on clouds. Hayden loved her and he'd asked her to marry him. If she had her way, she'd be shouting it from the top of Copper Mountain, but they'd agreed to wait before they told everyone. There was a little boy they had to talk to first.

From what Hayden had told her, it was clear the family had still been grieving Walker's untimely death when Madeline fell ill. She now better understood his reaction when she'd ended up in a ditch.

Her mom's death had taught her about grief. It was a process. Some days you could go about your daily tasks without thinking about it and on other days, when you least expect it, it grabbed you at the throat. It would be the same for Hayden. She knew and accepted that.

When they'd all finished lunch, Arlene got up. "Becket, Cooper, and Willow, you are the cleaning crew today. Luke, why don't you show Miss Anderson the books I've bought you? I think she has something she wants to tell you, too. Hayden, come with me, please?"

As they all got up, Hayden leaned over to her. "You want to talk to Luke alone, or do you want to wait for me?"

Before she could answer, Luke tugged at her hand. "I just want to know if I can now call you 'Mom'?"

Everyone fell silent. Hayden crouched down in front of his son. "That means she's going to be staying with us. Are you okay with that?"

Luke rolled his eyes. "I know that. You're going to marry her."

A collective gasp went up before Willow rushed closer and threw her arms around them. "I'm so happy for you guys!"

Grinning, Hayden shook his head. "Do I even have to ask how you all know?"

Cooper slapped him on the back. "You know we know. Congratulations, bro—I'm happy for you." He pulled Laura into a hug. "He messes with you, you come to me, okay?"

Then Becket was there, a huge grin on his face. "Now I understand why my lines didn't work on you." Again, she was enveloped in a bear hug.

Tears clogging up her throat, she turned to Arlene. The older woman opened her arms. "The only thing that would make me happier than this moment"—the older woman sniffed, hugging Laura—"is to hear that my other three children have also found love."

"Dream on, Mama," Becket teased as he gathered the plates on the table. "Not falling into that trap."

Grinning, Cooper kissed his mother's cheek. "You know I prefer animals."

"You can't marry them!" Arlene cried.

Cooper was already walking toward the kitchen. "Exactly!"

Laughing, Willow followed her brothers. "One out of four ain't bad, Mama," she drawled.

"You wanted to talk to me?" Hayden asked his mother when they were alone.

"Will you excuse us, Laura?" Arlene asked.

"Of course. Luke—come on and show me the books your grandma gave you."

Minutes later, she was lying on her tummy next to Luke, reading him a story. Molly and Jessie were stretched out next to them. The story was one of her favorites. By the time she closed the book, Luke was lying on his arms, his eyes closed, breathing deeply.

Her heart melted. She had indeed fallen in love with this little boy even before she'd met his dad. Combing his hair out of his face, she kissed his cheek.

"Mom," he murmured softly with a deep sigh.

Tears gathered behind her eyes. She would probably make many mistakes, but she would make sure he'd always know how very much she loved him.

Trying not to disturb him, she sat up. A movement from the door caught her eye. Hayden was leaning against the frame, watching them. Her heart tripped. With a quick glance to make sure Luke was okay, she hurried over to him.

He took her hand. "He'll be okay. Come with me?"

She followed him to the living room. Laughter and voices could be heard from the direction of the kitchen.

Hayden closed the door behind them before he turned to her. "I have something for you. If you don't like it or if it doesn't fit, I'll drive into Bozeman tomorrow...I was going to do that anyway. I can get you another one in any case—"

Smiling, she grabbed his hands. "What are you talking about?"

"The ring," he said, frowning, as if he'd been making perfect sense.

"What ring?"

Grinning sheepishly, he patted his pocket. "I forget everything when I'm with you." He took out a small box, a bit frayed at the edges. "This was my grandma's ring, Mom's mom. You would've liked her. She had spunk—like you have." Opening the box, he held it toward her.

Laura's breath caught in her throat. On a bed of black velvet was a cluster ring in a delicate vintage setting. Smaller diamonds were grouped around a central big diamond, creating a dazzling and radiant effect.

Putting out her hand, she touched it. "It's gorgeous. Will you put it on?"

"You like it?"

She couldn't stop the tears if she tried. "I love it. I love that it's part of your family."

He wiped a tear away with his thumb. "And the tears?"

"Because I'm so happy."

"So am I," he said huskily, slipping the ring on her finger. It fit. Perfectly. "This makes you my fiancée and part of our family."

Staring at her ring, she swallowed. "I haven't realized how much I've missed being part of a family until I met you guys."

The door flew open. "Can we now please pop the bubbly?" Willow laughed as Hayden's family gathered around them.

Her family too. She teared up again.

Hayden pulled her close, his familiar scent filling her senses. A perfect moment.

"You'll marry me any day, anywhere—that's what you said, isn't it?" Hayden asked.

"Yes, but…"

"Just checking." He grinned before he kissed her.

Whatever did he mean? But he deepened the kiss and she leaned into him. Nothing else mattered.

Chapter Twenty

Okay, this was now officially ridiculous. Hayden threw his phone on the bed. He was beat. Tired didn't begin to describe the bone-deep exhaustion he experienced. It was a busy time on the ranch, they rarely slept. He wasn't complaining about the lack of sleep or the hard work—that came with having a ranch. The reason for the frustration gnawing at his insides was because he rarely saw his fiancée.

It was the beginning of May, two months since he'd put his grandma's ring on Laura's finger, but he might as well still be single. Cold showers only helped up to a certain point. They saw one another once a week at the most and then neither of them wanted to talk. There were things to discuss, plans they had to make, but there was never time. When they were together, talking simply wasn't on his mind. He'd wanted to surprise her with a date for their wedding, but the days were too short to get everything done on the ranch, let alone organize a wedding.

For the past two months, he, Willow, Coop, and Becket even had to skip Sunday lunches as well. Calves didn't care for human schedules. Willow was also still busy with the last paintings for her upcoming exhibition, but she always helped during crazy times.

May meant they had to get the fences ready in the summer pastures. Branding lay ahead, a crazy busy time of year when all the ranchers helped each other. Bulls had to be tested, so that they would be sound for breeding. And soon they would move the cattle to the summer grass.

He wanted Laura here, with him. Even more, he needed her. It was also a busy time for her at school. He'd never really thought about a teacher's job, but listening to Laura, it seemed like ranching. Teaching was also a never-ending job.

So how the hell were they supposed to get married when nobody had time to organize a wedding? His phone rang. It was his mother. In that moment, a lightbulb flashed in his mind. Of course. Why hadn't he thought of it before?

"Mom, am I glad you phoned."

His mother laughed. "I'm no Willow, but I have been wondering about the wedding…"

"Exactly what I wanted to talk to you about."

"So, WHERE ARE we going again?" Laura asked, before hiding a yawn behind her hand. Going shopping on a Saturday was so not something she had time for right now, but Arlene and Willow simply wouldn't take no for an answer. Feeling guilty because she'd seen so little of her future mother-in-law and sister-in-law, she finally agreed.

To be honest, she'd much rather have spent the day with Hayden. She wanted to be his wife, live with him, share his bed every single day, not just if and when they had time. How were they supposed to fit a wedding in around ranching and seasons and people, though? Her own crazy schedule at school didn't help, either. Maybe when schools broke in the beginning of June, they could make time.

Willow parked her truck. "It's a surprise, but I promise you, you're going to love it. Ellie, I'm so glad you've joined us."

"I haven't really been anywhere since I've arrived in Marietta," Ellie said as she got out of the truck. "I've never been to Bozeman. It's a beautiful city." Turning around, she sighed. "Look at those mountains—I'll never get enough of looking at them."

Arlene took Laura's arm. "That's why Bozeman is called the Queen of the Rockies. You should come for a weekend. The historic districts and museums are really something. But today…drumroll…we are shopping for wedding dresses."

Laura gasped. "What? But…"

"I know." Arlene smiled. "You haven't set a date yet, and you're both working long hours and rarely see each other. That's why I thought we should start by trying on wedding dresses today. We are just looking," she added quickly as Laura opened her mouth to object. "Come on."

Swallowing her sigh, Laura traipsed behind Arlene and

Willow. Ellie was looking wide-eyed at everything.

By the time Arlene steered Laura into the third wedding shop, she was ready to drop. She was so tired she couldn't see straight. And honestly—the wedding dresses they'd seen so far were ghastly. It wasn't as if she had a very specific idea of what she wanted, but she knew she'd prefer more dress and less skin than what most of the dresses they'd seen so far seemed to go for.

"Aah, Mom—you should've brought us here first," cried Willow, and she rushed forward to touch a beautiful dress in a soft watermelon color. "Look at this one."

"That would look gorgeous with your red hair," Arlene said.

"It would, wouldn't it?" sighed Willow. "A pity I'm never getting married."

"Try it on, anyway." Arlene smiled. "Come on, Laura. Let's see what we can find for you."

The friendly saleslady approached them. "How may I help you today?"

"We have a bride-to-be," said Arlene before introducing everyone. "I hope you can help us. The dresses we've seen so far… let's just say, they are not what we're looking for."

"Well, you've come to the right place. My name is Josie and it would be my pleasure to help you. Why don't you sit down? I'll ask my assistant to get us some mimosas while you tell me what you like. How does that sound?"

"Perfect." With a deep sigh, Laura sank down on the

nearest chair. Her feet were throbbing.

"There we go. Up with the feet," Josie ordered as she pushed an ottoman under Laura's legs. She took a chair opposite the bride-to-be and, cocking her head, just looked at her for a few moments.

The bubbly arrived and after one sip, Laura felt her shoulders relax for the first time in days.

Josie asked her a few questions before she got up. "Okay, I think I know what you'll like."

"Willow?" Arlene called and leaned forward to see where her daughter was.

The door to one of the fitting rooms opened and Willow stepped out. She was wearing the dress she'd been admiring. "What do you think?" she asked, saucily placing a hand on her hip.

"Oh, sweetie, that is the perfect dress for you." Arlene sighed. "Now we just need to find you a husband."

Willow rolled her eyes. "Seriously, Mom." Quickly, she turned around.

"She does look gorgeous, doesn't she?" Ellie said. "Marriage is definitely also not in my future, but these are gorgeous dresses."

Both she and Arlene got up and walked toward the racks filled with wedding dresses in shades of white, cream, gray, pink, and even blue.

Arlene took down one in the palest of blues. "What about this one?" she asked. "Go on, try it on. It will look gorgeous with your blue eyes and blonde hair. We have all day. It'll be fun!" She smiled as Ellie hesitated.

Grinning, Ellie took the dress. "Okay, maybe I should see what I look like in a wedding dress, seeing that I'm never going to wear one for real."

"Laura?" Josie asked behind her.

Laura turned in her chair.

"What about something like this?" Josie asked and held out the dress she was carrying.

Laura's heart sighed and she slowly got up. Josie was holding a stunning white dress in satin. The top crossed in front in such a way that the sleeves would drop down her shoulders. Classy, stylish, and with a touch of vintage. "It's perfect. We haven't set a date yet, but when we do, I'll come back for this one." She took the dress. "Arlene, look—this is so pretty—what do you think?"

"It's beautiful. Go and try it on. Josie, do you have shoes for that dress? I'd love to see the whole picture."

Josie grinned, clearly excited. "Yes, we do. Just a moment."

A few minutes later, Laura stared at herself in the mirror, blinking back tears. She would've given anything to have her mom here today.

"May I come in?" asked Arlene from outside.

Laura wiped her eyes and opened the door.

Arlene took her hands. "Oh, Laura..." she sniffed. "I'm going to cry. You're perfect for my son. And this...wow—

this is the dress." She stroked Laura's arm. "You miss your mom?"

"I do," Laura said, her throat tight.

"Come on out!" called Willow from outside. "We also want to see."

Arlene gave Laura a hug before she opened the door.

Laura turned and posed as everyone admired the dress. There probably wouldn't be time to get married before next winter, but it was fun trying on wedding dresses, anyway.

"Well, I think this has been a successful trip," Arlene smiled. "Thanks for humoring me, Laura. Go put your clothes on. I'm taking you all to lunch!"

They found a restaurant not far from the bridal shop. It was only when Laura saw the menu that she realized how hungry she was. There hadn't been time this week for a proper meal.

Arlene's phone rang and she left the table.

"Have you eaten here before?" Ellie asked Willow. "What do you suggest?"

As they decided on what to eat, Laura leaned back in her chair. This had been a good idea. She'd been so busy at school. While she was still playing catch-up with the kids in her class, there was always something else going on too. She loved working with the kids and she loved her job, but it meant seeing less and less of Hayden.

He had warned her in the beginning how busy it always was on a ranch. She tried not to complain, but she missed him something fierce.

"Where's Arlene?" Ellie asked when their drinks arrived.

"Probably still on the phone," Willow said, her face hidden by the menu. "So what are we eating?"

THE NEXT FRIDAY morning, Hayden stood outside the homestead, grinning. They'd done it. With the help of the cowboys on their ranch as well as their neighbors, they'd converted the lawn in front of his house into a wedding venue. His mom had found a catering business who had put up a stretched tent, brought chairs, and who would also do tomorrow's catering. There were flowers everywhere—also thanks to his mother. They'd been working nonstop the whole week.

Willow walked closer. "It looks perfect, bro. I'm not sure how we've done it with everything else going on, but you have a wedding venue. And your bride has a dress, even though she doesn't know it yet." She laughed.

"Thank you for helping Mom with that," he grinned. "Everything okay for tonight?"

"Everything is perfect. I will let you know when we're on our way to Grey's Saloon. It is, after all, the place where you first saw her."

Shaking his head, Hayden grinned. "You know about that?"

"Of course I do. You just make sure you guys are on time."

FRIDAY NIGHT, LAURA parked her car in front of Ellie's Yarn Cove. It was raining and miserable outside. She missed Hayden. He was working again tonight and said he couldn't see her. All she wanted was something to eat and her bed, but her friends had other ideas. For some reason or other, the book club had been moved to tonight, and all her excuses were ignored.

Wearily, she got out of her car and walked toward Ellie's shop. The soft drizzle had her hurrying.

Strange. The place was dark. She peered through the glass door, but couldn't see anything. Maybe they were in the back? Or had she completely misunderstood Arlene?

Sighing, she tried the door. It opened. Okay, so that meant…

As she stepped inside, the lights came on.

"Surprise!" yelled the whole book club, each with a glass of bubbly in hand.

Laura was so flabbergasted, she couldn't get a word out.

Arlene, with a bride's veil in her hands, walked up to her. "You better brace yourself, sweetheart, there are a few more shockers in store for you tonight. This is the first one. You've just arrived at your kitchen tea/bachelorette party/whatever."

Dazed, Laura stared at her friends as Arlene put the veil on her head.

"Come on, get your coat off." Willow laughed. "We have presents for you!"

A wonderful warm feeling spread throughout Laura's body. And to think she'd been so miserable. There was so much to be grateful for. Not only was she engaged to a gorgeous cowboy and had become part of his family, but she'd also found the most wonderful friends.

Laughing, she hugged Arlene. "So that's why you didn't want a lift tonight. I suppose everyone in town knows by now Hayden and I are engaged?"

"Everyone already knew by Sunday night." Arlene grinned.

"I told you about this town," Maria said. "Everyone knows everything. I heard the news Monday morning before school."

Laura shook her head. "I was wondering how everyone at school knew about it."

"Well," Arlene said, "Carol Bingley phoned me on Sunday evening to confirm the rumor."

Laura groaned. "We only got engaged on Sunday!"

Janice patted her arm. "It's Marietta, my dear. Everyone knows everything."

"We are leaving for Grey's Saloon after you've opened your presents." Willow smiled. "I cannot tell you how happy I am that one of my siblings is getting married. Mom will hopefully stop pestering me about getting a husband."

"Well, you never know." Janice grinned. "This is Marietta, after all. Anything can happen."

Smiling, Ellie gave Laura a glass of bubbly. "Cheers, Laura. I'm so happy for you. Good men are few and far between, but from what I've heard in town, you've struck gold."

Annie also came closer for a hug. "I like to think Annie's is the reason why you and Hayden got together. If you and your friend hadn't stayed with us on your way to Yellowstone National Park, you may never have fallen in love with Marietta!"

Laughing, Vivian raised her glass. "To Marietta and Copper Mountain. There is a certain kind of magic at work here, whether you're looking for it or not."

Sniffing, Laura dug into her pocket for a tissue. "I can't stop crying! I'm so happy. It's so dreary outside, but then you guys…"

Behind them, the door of the shop flew open. They all turned around. A very wet, shivering woman entered. For a moment, she stared at them before she burst into tears.

Laura's protective instincts kicked in and she rushed closer. "Hello, I'm Laura," she said softly as she took the woman's arm. "Come on in. You look cold."

"Here," Riley said as she approached them with a towel in hand. "Let's get you out of that wet jacket."

HAYDEN KEPT LOOKING at his watch. What on earth was keeping the women? It was nearly nine o'clock. Maybe he should've spoken to Laura first and told her what they'd been doing. Springing a surprise like this one on her after a busy week was maybe not such a bright idea, after all.

"Heard anything?" Cooper asked.

Hayden took out his phone. "I'm going to phone..."

"There they are," Becket called out, pointing toward the door.

His mom, Willow, Vivian, Annie, Janice, and Maria all stood in the doorway, looking for them.

He hastened closer. "Where's Laura? Why are you so late?"

His mother hugged him. "We had a bit of a hiccup. Nothing we gals couldn't handle, so don't worry. Laura will tell you all about it. She's just in the bathroom. You've found yourself a lovely wife, son. She's got a big heart. We'll wait for you at the table."

What hiccup? Was Laura having second thoughts? Frowning, he hurried to the bathrooms.

As he approached, the ladies' room door opened and Laura stepped out. A beautiful smile lit up her face when she saw him. His heart settled. Everything was okay. Whatever problem there was, they'd talk about it and figure it out together.

Relieved, he took her hand. "Hey, beautiful. You passing through town?"

She batted her eyelashes while moving closer to him. "Well, I don't know. I could decide to stay. Depends on what you have to offer."

"Marry me?"

Laughing, she leaned into him. "I've already said yes, remember?"

"And you said any place, any time?"

Slowly, she looked up. "Yes, but…"

"I miss you. It'll make more sense to wait until winter when we're not so busy, but I want you… I need you with me. There are still things we need to figure out, I know. Do you want to keep your house? Are you happy to drive into town every day, because we won't mind staying with you…"

Surprised, she stared at him. "You'd do that?"

"From tomorrow, I'm never going to be apart from you again."

"What happens tomorrow?" She smiled.

"We're getting married."

With his breath in his throat, he watched every emotion on her face—surprise, worry, and finally joy. "Really?"

"Really."

"I don't have a dress…"

"It's hanging in our room on the ranch."

Frowning, she angled her head. "I don't understand. What is…" Her eyes widened. "Your mother?"

"My mother. She bought it last Saturday while you were having lunch."

"I can pay for—"

He quickly put a finger on her lips. "I know, but let me do this for you, please?"

Slipping her fingers in his hair, she pulled his head down for a slow kiss. They were both breathless when she moved her head back. "So tell me about this wedding."

"Everyone pitched in. Willow, all your friends, my family, neighbors, just about everyone in town."

"We're getting married tomorrow?"

"Yes, please?"

"What can I do?"

"Show up."

"I can't wait."

Of course, he had to kiss her again. "I can't take you away for a honeymoon at the moment, but—"

It was her turn to put a finger on his lips. "I just want to be with you."

Grinning, he pulled her closer. "It seems I was right all along."

"About what?"

"Turns out, you're not so averse to sweaty cowboys as you once thought."

"I've discovered I love it. Kiss me, cowboy," she demanded before she pulled his head down.

His heart finally settled. She was here, with him. The rest they'd sort out along the way. Together.

Chapter Twenty-One

GROGGILY, LAURA OPENED her eyes. There were strange sounds coming from the direction of the kitchen. She quickly sat up. It took a few moments before the events of the previous night came flooding back. Rose had to be up. Molly was nowhere to be seen; she was probably also in the kitchen. Grabbing a top, she headed out of her room.

The woman who'd arrived at Ellie's Yarn Cove last night—wet, shivering, and crying—was named Rose Dalton. That was all they'd gotten out of her last night. They'd brought her back to Laura's home. It was probably crazy to open your house to a stranger, but there had been something so vulnerable in the poor woman's eyes, she didn't have the heart to leave her alone at a hotel or any other place.

Rose was standing in front of the window, a mug of coffee in her hand. She looked like a completely different woman from the one they'd seen last night, though. For one, she was dry, a cascade of red hair hanging down her back. She was wearing the track suit Laura had lent her the previous night. Molly was sitting at her feet. When the dog saw Laura, she got up and, tail wagging, ran over to her.

Bending down, she scratched Molly's ears. Rose still hadn't heard her. "Good morning, Rose," Laura said softly.

Rose turned around.

"Your hair…"

Grimacing, Rose touched her red tresses. "Red hair and freckles, I know."

"I was going to say you're gorgeous. Your hair was so wet last night, I didn't see the color. I'm so sorry we had to leave you alone last night, but…" Laura lifted her hand. "I got engaged a while back, but we've been so busy, there hadn't been time to talk about the wedding. Turns out, my fiancé organized everything. We're getting married today!"

Rose blinked. "Wow. That's—"

"Crazy? Different?" Laura laughed. "So is this town." Watching Rose, she poured herself a mug of coffee as well. "Where are you heading?"

Rose turned back from the window and sat down at the table. "I don't really know. I just…I had to get away. I got in my car and put my foot on the gas. Somewhere along the highway, I saw the words, 'Montana' and 'Yellowstone River.' I've just watched a series set here, so I kept going. My car…I nearly ended up in a ditch last night, some crazy cowboy yelled at me…I think something is wrong with the tires—" Clearly overwhelmed, she wiped her eyes. "I've been so stupid."

Laura pulled out a chair and sat next to Rose. "You know what I've discovered in Marietta? Oh, the gossip mill is astounding, but people also care for each other around here. We noticed you had a flat tire. Someone is picking up your car this morning and you'll have it back later today. I'm just amazed that you were able to drive into town with a flat tire."

"It was raining, so I was going slow. But to tell you the truth, I don't know anything about cars. Well…" she sighed. "I actually don't know anything, I've come to realize. It's all such a mess—" Tears rolled down her cheeks again.

"Rose, I'm going with my gut here. We don't know each other, but you're obviously going through something at the moment. I have a proposition for you. As I've said, I'm getting married today, so I'm moving to the ranch. Well, the 'moving' will probably not happen today, but during the next few weeks. I haven't yet decided what to do with this house. Why don't you stay here until you've figured out what you want to do? If you need to borrow money, I'm happy to help…"

Rose shook her head. "I've got money, thanks. That, at least, isn't a problem. Thanks, Laura. Maybe if I could stay for the weekend?"

"Of course. And really, there is no hurry. I teach at the local elementary school and will probably come around every afternoon to take stuff out to the ranch, but we'll keep in touch." Laura hesitated for a moment. She didn't want to intrude, but this was important, so she was going to just ask. "Do you need to let your family know where you are? I'm just worried a search party is out looking for you."

Shaking her head, Rose wiped her eyes again. "Don't worry. Nobody will miss me."

Laura put her mug down. Arlene was picking her up in a little while, but she felt so bad leaving Rose alone. "Why don't you come to the wedding this afternoon? I can ask one of my future brothers-in-law if they'll bring you back?"

Rose shook her head. "Thank you, but I'll be okay. I'll probably just sleep." Molly jumped up against her legs. Bending down, Rose picked her up. "Do you think…Molly can stay with me? She was so great last night."

Laura smiled. "Let's ask her. Molly, what do you say?" Laura smiled.

Molly licked Rose's face. For the first time, Rose smiled. Two dimples appeared on either side of her face.

Laura scratched Molly's ears. "I think that was a yes. Rose, I don't want to intrude, but do you have a bag with you? I gave you something to sleep in last night…"

Rose shook her head. "No bag. But don't worry about me, please…oh, my car…"

"We're about the same size, I think. Please take anything you need from my closet, okay? But now I must get ready. Are you sure you'll be okay? I'll pop in on Monday to get some of my things. There should be enough food in the fridge until next week."

Rose got up with Molly in her arms. "I don't know how to thank you. I'll…I promise I'll tell you what happened but—"

Laura touched her shoulder. "Whenever you're ready."

A FAMILY WITH THE COWBOY

JUST BEFORE THE sun set, Hayden stood next to his brothers, waiting for his bride. All of them had wet hair, as they'd all just arrived in the tent. Ranch work never stopped for long, not even for a wedding.

It had been a crazy day with a thousand last-minute things that had to be done besides the normal ranch chores. Luke was also supposed to have joined them, but according to Becket, his son was with their mother.

He couldn't wait to see Laura, to begin a life together with her. Early this morning, he'd been to Madeline's grave. All he'd felt was peace. He'd had a good life with Maddie, even though they'd been so young when they'd gotten married. She'd given him a son, whose smile and zest for life would always remind him of her and of how happy they'd been.

It was time to leave the past behind him, though. He'd fallen in love again. This time round, love had arrived with a passion that left him breathless every time he laid eyes on Laura. He didn't think he'd ever get enough of her.

"What's the story about the woman who stumbled into the shop where the women were last night?" Cooper asked.

Hayden shrugged. "Nobody seems to know where she came from. She's staying in Laura's house for a while."

"I wonder if it's the same woman I found…"

A music note filled the air and Cooper fell silent. Willow

and Ellie appeared at the entrance of the tent. He'd only met Ellie this morning. Apparently, she'd opened the yarn shop in town where they were having their monthly book club meetings.

"Who's the blonde?" asked Becket.

"A friend of Laura's," Hayden said. "She's the one who has opened a shop in town…"

"Why haven't I seen her before?" Becket wanted to know.

But Hayden had stopped listening. As Ellie and Willow joined them in the front, his mother walked in, nodding and smiling at everybody before she took her seat.

When he turned his gaze back to the opening of the tent, Laura appeared, hand in hand with Luke. Tears gathered behind his eyes. This picture he'd carry with him to his grave. Luke, in a suit with a bow tie, proudly walked next to his "Mom," as he'd been calling her all day.

Laura was a beautiful woman, but today, she looked exquisite. Her wedding dress was cut in such a way that her shoulders were bare and all he could think about was sliding his lips over the velvety texture of her skin. The delicate chain with a diamond pendant he'd left for her on their bed was around her neck. A vivid image of her wearing nothing else but that had him just about hyperventilating.

His body responded. Damn, this was going to be a long day.

A FAMILY WITH THE COWBOY

BY THE TIME all the speeches were done, Laura was burning up. She couldn't wait to be alone with her handsome bridegroom. His arm was lying behind her on her chair, his hand either playing with her hair or drawing circles on her skin.

They'd eaten, but she had no idea what. People had come up to them to congratulate them. She'd smiled and nodded, but wouldn't be able to repeat a single word. All she'd been acutely aware of the entire evening was Hayden's warm hand against her back, his steady presence by her side.

"Dance with me?" Hayden said and held out his hand.

The band was playing, but she hadn't even noticed. "Yes, please." She smiled as she got up.

The guests cheered as Hayden led them to the dance floor. The music changed and she laughed. "It's the kissing song!"

"It's our song." He smiled as they glided over the floor.

Other couples joined them and soon just about everyone was on the floor.

"You've got moves, Cowboy." She grinned as she easily followed his steps. "And you do kiss me like I've never been kissed before."

"Dancing with you is like making love to you," he whispered in her ear. "You know exactly what I want."

And just like that, passion was burning low in her belly. "How long do we have to stay? I'm about to burst into flames…I can't wait to be with you."

His eyes darkened and with his jaw clenched, he steered her out of the tent.

"Hayden…"

Grabbing her hand, he ran toward the house. "We'll be back, but you're not the only one ready to explode."

The house was a beehive of waiters moving in and out. Cussing under his breath, Hayden quickly led her to the stairs. Before she realized what he was going to do, he'd picked her up in his arms and was taking the stairs two at a time.

Seconds later, he'd locked the bedroom door and was pulling down the top of her dress. Her breasts sprang free, he dropped his head, and with a growl, he fastened his mouth around a throbbing nipple.

Leaning with her back against the cool wall, her fingers slid into his hair, and she held him close to her. But she was too hungry for him. It had been too long.

"Hayden…" she moaned. "I need you…"

With his eyes on her, his breath ragged, he got rid of his pants before he lifted her dress, his hands gliding up and up her legs. His hand stopped and he smiled—a wicked one that had her knees wobbling. "No panties?"

"Not with the dress." She pulled him closer. "Now, Hayden, now."

"Yes, Mrs. Weston," he said, slipping into her. "Happy to oblige."

A FAMILY WITH THE COWBOY

Stars exploded behind her eyes, and as they took that wild ride together, she held on tightly.

By the time they returned outside, most of the guests had left.

"Don't worry, bro," Becket said. "We didn't even have to explain. Everybody knew what you were up to."

His mother shook her head. "I'm sure by now Carol Bingley is already spreading the news."

Laura had covered her cheeks with her hands. "This town—I don't know if I'll ever get used to the gossip!" She looked around. "Has Ellie left? I've wanted to thank her."

"She left right after the ceremony," Willow said. "When the first cowboy headed her way to ask her to dance, she was out of here."

"Interesting," Becket said.

"From the little she's said about herself," Arlene said, "it's clear she has no interest in getting involved with anyone. A pity. She's a beauty. But you never know…"

Groaning, Willow grabbed her mom's arm. "Come on, Mom. Let's get you home before you start planning the next wedding."

"Yours, I hope?" Arlene grinned.

"Mo-o-m!" Willow rolled her eyes before she turned away. "Luke!" she called. "Come on, we're leaving!"

"I've booked a table for us at the Graff tomorrow," said Becket. "My treat. You lovebirds are also welcome to join, but I'm sure—"

Hayden put his arms around Laura's shoulders. "We'll be busy."

Just then, Luke came running toward them, Jessie at his heels. "I'm staying with Grandma till Monday," he said as he grabbed Laura's hand. "I'll miss you, Mom."

Laura crouched down and hugged him. Hayden had to swallow against the lump in his throat. Look at them—his wife, his son, his family.

Laura got up and, with his arm around her, they waved their family good-bye.

"So, Mrs. Weston, I don't know about you, but right now, I only have one thing on my mind."

Turning in his arms, she laughed. "If it involves getting naked, I'm in."

Picking her up, he strode toward the front door. "That's exactly what I was thinking."

Slipping her arms around his neck, she smiled. "So this is what happens when you fall for a cowboy?"

Holding her close, he took the stairs two at a time. "Exactly."

The End

If you enjoyed *A Family With the Cowboy*,
you'll love the next book in…

The Westons of Montana series

Book 1: *A Family With the Cowboy*

Book 2: *Reckless with the Cowboy*

Available now at your favorite online retailer!

Acknowledgements

I will forever be grateful that I met Jane Porter while she visited South Africa a few years ago. Listening to her road to publication was what inspired me to keep on writing after several rejections. Thanks to the whole Tule team for also liking this series—it's just a pleasure working with all of you. A special thanks to Kelly Hunter who has been the editor for this series as well—she has such a gentle, encouraging manner, making the whole process such a joy.

I also want to thank fellow Tule author Jeannie Watt, who went out of her way explaining all things *Montana* and ranch to me.

Thank you again, dear reader, for picking up this story—I hope you enjoy reading about the Westons of Montana!

And as always, thanks to my husband Theo, who is always cheering me on.

More Books by Elsa Winckler

The Millers of Marietta series
Book 1: *My Montana Valentine*

Book 2: *A Match Made in Montana*

Book 3: *Merry Christmas, Montana*

The Cavallo Brothers series
Book 1: *An Impossible Attraction*

Book 2: *An Irresistible Temptation*

Book 3: *The Ultimate Surrender*

Other Title
Where the River Bends

Available now at your favorite online retailer!

About the Author

Elsa has been reading love stories for as long as she can remember and when she 'met' the classic authors like Jane Austen, Elizabeth Gaskell, Henry James, the Brontë sisters, etc. during her Honors studies, she was hooked for life.

Although her three gown-up children rarely acknowledge the fact they have a romance-writing mom, her husband fortunately, is very proud of her, reads every word and is happy to make sure she gets the kissing scenes just right.

She likes the heroines in her stories to be beautiful, feisty, independent and headstrong. And the heroes must be strong but possess a generous amount of sensitivity. They are of course, also gorgeous. Her stories typically incorporate the family background of the characters to better understand where they come from and who they are when we meet them in the story.

Thank you for reading

A Family With the Cowboy

If you enjoyed this book, you can find more from all our great authors at TulePublishing.com, or from your favorite online retailer.

Made in the USA
Middletown, DE
28 June 2025